Falling in Love

"Chelsea." He had a way of saying my name that made it sound different. His hands were on my shoulders, and when he kissed me again it wasn't gentle or sweet. Over the pulse buzzing in my ears I heard faint, unfamiliar warning bells. I could feel the smooth brown skin of his back beneath my fingernails and the hot sun on my bare arms. Dimly I registered the fact that I wanted to get closer, and it was this thought that finally made me pull away.

"I'm sorry," Jess whispered thickly. "I hope you don't . . ."

"I'm not sorry. . . ."

You'll Love These New Titles from Vista

(0451)

☐ **PLEASE DON'T KISS ME NOW by Merrill Joan Gerber.** With her mom into self-fulfillment and her dad remarried, life for fifteen-year-old Leslie is getting pretty confusing. And when Brian Sweeney, the senior-class heartthrob starts getting interested in her she tries to forget her troubles and find security in his arms . . .   (115759—$1.95)

☐ **CALL ME MARGO by Judith St. George.** Margo Allinger's family moved around so much that the shy teenager could never make any lasting friendships. But now she was going to be living at Haywood for three whole years. At first everything goes well, but when the going gets tough Margo realizes that it is up to her to conquer her fear and learn to speak up for herself.   (118502—$2.25)

☐ **TWO POINT ZERO by Anne Snyder and Louis Pelletier.** If Kate Fleming hadn't desperately needed the money for college, she never would have agreed to write papers for the football team's star kicker. Everything goes smoothly until she gets involved with handsome Doug Hollis, whose exposée on cheating for the magazine threatens to ruin her chances for getting into law school.   (114760—$1.75)

☐ **TWO LOVES FOR JENNY by Sandy Miller.** When Jenny and her boyfriend Doug both enter the statewide music competition she is faced with a tough choice: should she let Doug win, or should she play her best, and possibly lose his friendship instead?   (115317—$1.75)

Prices slightly higher in Canada

Buy them at your local bookstore or use this convenient coupon for ordering.

NEW AMERICAN LIBRARY,
P.O. Box 999, Bergenfield, New Jersey 07621

Please send me the books I have checked above. I am enclosing $_____ (please add $1.00 to this order to cover postage and handling). Send check or money order—no cash or C.O.D.'s. Prices and numbers are subject to change without notice.

Name_____

Address_____

City_____State_____Zip Code_____
Allow 4-6 weeks for delivery.
This offer is subject to withdrawal without notice.

The Princess Routine

by

Tonya Wood

A SIGNET VISTA BOOK
NEW AMERICAN LIBRARY

PUBLISHER'S NOTE

This novel is a work of fiction. Names, characters, places, and
incidents either are the product of the author's imagination or are
used fictitiously, and any resemblance to actual persons, living or dead,
events, or locales is entirely coincidental.

NAL BOOKS ARE AVAILABLE AT QUANTITY DISCOUNTS WHEN USED TO PROMOTE
PRODUCTS OR SERVICES. FOR INFORMATION PLEASE WRITE TO PREMIUM
MARKETING DIVISION, NEW AMERICAN LIBRARY, 1633 BROADWAY, NEW YORK,
NEW YORK 10019.

RL/5/IL 5+

Copyright©1985 by Tonya Wood

All rights reserved

SIGNET VISTA TRADEMARK REG.U.S.PAT.OFF. AND FOREIGN COUNTRIES
REGISTERED TRADEMARK—MARCA REGISTRADA
HECHO EN CHICAGO, U.S.A.

SIGNET, SIGNET CLASSIC, MENTOR, PLUME, MERIDIAN and NAL BOOKS
are published by New American Library,
1633 Broadway, New York, New York 10019

First Printing, November, 1985

1 2 3 4 5 6 7 8 9

PRINTED IN THE UNITED STATES OF AMERICA

For my father,
Harold D. Glazier

*His life was gentle, and the elements
so mixed in him that Nature might stand
up and say to all the world: This was
a man.*
—Julius Caesar, Act V

Chapter 1

"Your brother is a nerd," Sandy stated flatly.

I had been aware of this fact for nearly ten years, ever since the memorable day when my twin brother, Rick, had made sandwich filling in the blender using my guppies. It was somewhat surprising that my next-door neighbor and lifelong friend had reached the ripe old age of seventeen before discovering the sad truth. Normally Sandy DeSpain was pretty quick on the uptake.

"So what else is new?" I stifled a yawn, being very careful not to smear my wet nail polish. The color was fantastic, a brilliant hot pink that was guaranteed to glow in the dark. I had shut myself in the closet and verified this claim just minutes before. "Rick is a nerd, today is Thursday, and the sun will set tonight in the west. The simple and indisputable facts of life. Do you think I should paint little white flowers on my nails or put glitter on the tips?"

Sandy groaned and threw herself back into the ruffled pillows on my canopy bed, grabbing one of the stuffed animals I had treasured since my diaper days. I winced from my vantage point on the window seat as she slowly choked the life out of Winnie-the-Pooh.

"He makes me crazy," Sandy wailed. "Other boys like me. I've even been told that I'm reasonably attractive. I shower regularly, brush my teeth three times a day, love pets and children. What more could any boy want? You'd think that after knowing me for an entire lifetime the turkey would recognize what a prize I am. What am I doing wrong, Chelsea?"

"I'll tell you," I said, "if you will stop abusing that innocent bear."

"Sorry." She released her stranglehold and straightened Winnie's crushed red ribbon.

"I hope you won't be offended when I tell you this." I leaned back in the cushioned seat, resting my head against the lace-trimmed window shade. "It's your perfume," I said simply.

Sandy looked dumbfounded, her eyebrows lost in fluffy brown bangs. "My perfume? I wear the same kind I've always worn—Irish Spring deodorant soap."

"Not good enough," I told her solemnly. "To attract Ranger Rick you'd have to wrap yourself in an animal hide and rub deer scent all over your body. Believe me, he'd be on your trail like a shot."

Unfortunately, truer words were never spoken. Rick's fascination with the rugged Rocky Mountains that surrounded our Denver, Colorado, home had long ago earned him his nickname, "Ranger." His greatest—and only—ambition in life was to graduate with a degree in forestry and become a ranger for the U.S. Forest Service. I have never understood how Rick can enjoy uncomfortable and unrewarding activities such as backpacking, hunting and fishing. Climbing some mountain just to climb down again, or tracking imaginary animals through insect-ridden forests is not my idea of a good time. I live life by a simple motto: Never walk when you can ride, and never sit when you can recline. I have the good fortune to be barely over five feet tall with curly blond hair and wide blue eyes. I suppose I give the impression of someone who might easily be broken. Call me a reject in the era of women's liberation, but I enjoy nothing more than being handled—figuratively speaking—like a delicate piece of china by a tall, broad-shouldered football player.

Sandy sighed heavily, pushing herself to a sitting position. Winnie-the-Pooh tumbled silently off the bed, landing headfirst on the plush, rose-colored carpet. "Deer scent, huh? Well, if I thought it would work, I'd try it. You know, it never ceases to amaze me that you and Ranger are even related, let alone twins. I've never met two people who are less alike. Ranger is this tall, dark-haired outdoors type, and you're a hothouse orchid. Your eyes aren't even the same color."

"That's because we're fraternal twins," I replied. "And it never ceases to amaze me that you are even interested in that overgrown boy scout. Anyone who wants to spend his adult life living with squirrels is just a little bit strange if you ask me. Did I tell you what he's doing next week? You won't believe this one."

"Try me." Sandy's tone indicated that there was nothing I could tell her about Ranger Rick that would be surprising.

"Running the Colorado River. Now tell me that isn't weird."

"I would," Sandy said slowly, "if I knew what it was."

"Have you ever heard of Calahan Expeditions?" I asked.

Sandy shrugged. "The name is familiar. Don't they sponsor that wilderness camp for underprivileged kids?"

"Apparently that's not all they do. Last year Ranger got to know some guy in school named Jess Calahan, whose father owns Calahan Expeditions. He told Ranger that they organize river trips down the Colorado every summer. Well, you know my adorable brother. He signed up on the spot."

"Jess Calahan . . ." Sandy frowned. "Wasn't he a senior, tall with kind of streaky blond hair?"

"I don't know, I never met him. Anyway, Nature Boy is leaving next Monday for five fun-filled days of bobbing up and down on a muddy river. I haven't seen him so excited since Dad bought him that Springbar tent for his birthday. Can you imagine a more thrilling way to spend the last week of summer vacation than getting sunburned and seasick on a little rubber raft?"

Sandy appeared to be taking my question seriously —very seriously. She was staring at the curtain above my head, as if the mysteries of the universe had suddenly been revealed in the pink-and-white gingham. A smile teased the corners of her eyes, and her mouth slowly curved upward.

"Miss DeSpain?" I clicked my hot-pink fingers in the air. "Hello? Are you there?"

"This river trip," Sandy murmured thoughtfully. "Can anyone sign up?"

"I suppose so." I frowned. "Anyone who is rowing with one oar out of the water. Why?"

Sandy's smile widened, catching me right in the solar plexus. "Sandy," I said softly, "you wouldn't be—you couldn't *possibly* be—thinking what I think you're thinking . . . are you?"

Sandy nodded happily. "It's perfect. Perfect! We sign up for the river trip, and I get five whole days to impress Ranger with my love of the great outdoors. Can't you see it? Those romantic star-filled nights, sitting around a crackling camp fire—"

"All I see," I snapped, "is a raving maniac in the middle of my canopy bed. You and I on a raft on the Colorado River? You're no more of an outdoorswoman than I am. We'd die of exposure the first day."

"Speak for yourself," Sandy replied indignantly. "I went camping with my folks last summer for an entire week and had a great time."

I shivered, as if hundreds of timber ants were already marching up and down my spine. "I'm very happy for you. But I do not camp. I don't even picnic. If you would really like to sign up for this river trip, more power to you. But count me out."

"But why?" Sandy scrambled off the bed, looming over me in the window seat. "My mom could get along without me at the pet shop for one week. And you only work at the Burger Barn on weekends. There's not a reason in the world we couldn't go."

This was very sad. My poor friend had cleaned out one too many gerbil cages.

"Not a reason in the world?" I asked. "I can think of one or two, just for starters. Let's see, there's indoor plumbing, hot and cold running water, my Serta Posture-Pedic mattress . . . need I go on?"

"You're being stubborn," Sandy said. "Stubborn and spoiled. You're missing out on the experience of a lifetime. What are mere creature comforts compared to that?"

"Bite your tongue. You are talking about my electric curlers."

"All right!" Sandy threw her hands in the air, her cheeks the same dusky rose as my carpet. "Then do it for your dearest and closest friend. I can't sign up alone. Ranger will think I'm chasing him."

"Don't let that bother you," I mumbed wryly. "You've been after that nitwit for five years, and he hasn't noticed yet."

Sandy opened her mouth and shut it again in a tight line. She glared at me in a very uncomfortable, accusing sort of way. I inched backward in the window seat and studied the brushed-gold pinkie ring on my finger.

"Well, I wouldn't want you to put yourself out," she said stiffly. "Forget I asked."

"Sandy, listen to me." I tried to keep my voice very calm. The sane pyschiatrist soothing a wacko lunatic.

"You don't know what a miserable experience this river trip will be. I've heard Ranger talking about it. There are mosquitoes as big as your fist, and if you fall into the river, all these tiny, vicious fish chew on your toes." This disgusting description was straight out of a jungle movie I'd seen, but who was to know? The hazards of a river trip were probably far worse than even I could imagine. "Can you really see us enjoying that sort of thing? In two weeks we're going to be slaving away at Skyview High. I don't want to spend my last days as a free woman with my head hung over the side of a rubber raft. There has got to be a better way to wind up our summer vacation than that."

"All right." Sandy's voice was very cool. "You've made your point. I do wonder how you've come to be such an expert on outdoor life when you've never even set foot outside the city limits. But I won't argue with you. Far be it from me to suggest you try something challenging. Consider the subject closed."

"Where are you going?" I followed Sandy across the room, shuffling my bare feet on the carpet. I felt like a first-class jerk, which was absurd. Sandy knew as well as I did that I was strictly the cream-puff type. I had already gone seventeen years without using an outhouse, and there was certainly no reason to start now.

"I'm going back to the shop," Sandy said. "Mom needs me to help close up. Don't bother walking me downstairs. You might strain a muscle or something."

The bedroom door opened and slammed in my face. It did not take a genius to figure out that Sandy was really steamed.

For a moment I considered going after her, telling her I had changed my mind and would go on the lousy river trip. But only for a moment.

Do without my blow dryer for five days? Who was I kidding?

*   *   *

That evening at dinner Mom unveiled her latest cooking effort, a meat loaf shaped like a daisy. Each petal was glazed with chili sauce, and the center was a heaping mound of mashed potatoes. My mother is a nutritionist at St. Benedict's Hospital, and food is her life. I am quite possibly the only teenage girl in Denver who still gets a Flintstones chewable vitamin each and every morning. She loves the cheery touch of color they add when placed next to a fluffy lemon-yellow omelet (her description, not mine).

Although I normally enjoy meat loaf, whatever its shape, tonight it stuck in my throat like dry leather. I was bored and irritable, and my thoughts kept straying to the argument I had had with Sandy. I couldn't decide who had been right and who had been wrong, so I finally pinned the blame on Ranger Rick. If he thought as much about the birds and the bees as he did about chipmunks and bears, he would have asked Sandy out ages ago, and the whole incident would never have happened. By the time desert was served I had worked myself into a fine temper. When Ranger reached across my plate for the water pitcher, I nastily told him that even a nerd could learn a few manners.

Instead of yelling back, which I had expected him to do, he chewed thoughtfully on his lemon Bundt cake. He finally swallowed and asked, "You and Sandy have a fight today?"

I eyed him suspiciously. "Why do you ask?"

"Just curious." He shrugged. "When she left here this afternoon, she looked kind of mad. Almost slammed my foot in the door."

"Chelsea?" It was my father, his interest piqued. My father is a corporate mediator, which is a fancy name for someone who solves arguments between labor and management. He flies all over the country and has made quite a name for himself. A little spat between Sandy and me was right up his alley. "Is it something you'd like to tell me about? Perhaps I can help."

Wonderful. Now everyone was staring at me, waiting for the gory details. I silently vowed to strangle my brother at the first opportunity.

"It's nothing," I said tightly. "A little disagreement. No big deal. I'll call her tonight and apologize."

"Apologize?" My mother picked up on that one very quickly. "What did you do to her?"

"Nothing! For Pete's sake, we're a little old to be pulling each other's pigtails! She had a stupid idea and I told her so, that's all. Any more questions?"

"What stupid idea?" Ranger asked innocently.

I took a deep breath and counted to ten. "Since you are so interested, I'll tell you. Sandy thought it might be fun to go along on that river trip you're taking next week."

It began as a deep rumbling, like distant thunder. Then Ranger erupted into unmistakable—and uncontrollable —laughter.

I looked at my father. He was smirking. Then I looked at my mother, whose water glass had stopped halfway to her mouth. I listened to Ranger's belly laughs until I couldn't stand it any longer.

"All right." I smiled stiffly at my brother, who was now convulsed on the dining room table. "I can see that you are all terribly amused. Do you mind telling me just what is so funny?"

"You have to be kidding," Ranger managed. "You and Sandy running the Colorado? No wonder you told her to forget it. You two wouldn't make it through the first day."

Although this was practically the same thing I had told Sandy, it sounded different coming from my brother. Like an insult.

"Dad?" I asked quietly.

The corporate mediator wiped the smile off his face, replacing it with a look of thoughtful consideration.

"Well," he said carefully, "I'd have to say I understand your position on this. Sandy obviously didn't realize what would be involved, or I'm sure she wouldn't have suggested it."

My mother, ever the diplomat, asked if anyone wanted more Bundt cake.

I looked at Rick. "Why don't you tell me what *is* involved? Just for curiosity's sake?"

"Oh, this and that," Rick said, drawling. "Little things like hanging on for dear life when you hit the rapids; sleeping on the cold, hard ground every night; cooking food without a microwave oven . . . nothing you two couldn't handle, I'm sure." He dropped his face into his hands and began howling like a hyena again.

I resisted the urge to pour the pitcher of water over his head. A far better idea had occurred to me.

"I've changed my mind," I said calmly. "I think Sandy and I will go on this river trip after all. It sounds like fun."

Revenge was sweet. Ranger lifted his head, gazing at me with startled gray eyes. "You're kidding."

"Oh, no. The three of us will have a great time together. Sandy and I will sign up first thing tomorrow."

My father cleared his throat. "Chelsa, dear . . . this isn't a decision to be made on the spur of the moment. I'm not sure you realize how difficult this river trip will be."

"If Ranger Rick can do it," I replied airily, "then I'm sure I can."

"Rick is a *boy*," said my father.

Words of war. Up until then I had had no intention of actually going through with my crazy declaration. The plan had been simply to put Ranger in his place. Suddenly my father's opinion had put a whole new perspective on things.

"Just what does that have to do with anything?" I said slowly.

"I'm going to be sick." Ranger groaned. "Mom, tell her. Do the kid a favor. Tell her she's nuts."

"Irene." Clearly my father felt in need of a little support. "Irene, we have a problem here. I would appreciate your input."

My mother began scraping crumbs off the table with her butter knife. She glanced at me sideways, and I knew that it was two against two.

"I had an opportunity to climb the Grand Teton once," she said. "Do you remember, Carl? It was the summer we got engaged. A group of students from the college went."

My father looked uncomfortable. "Honey, I hardly think this is the time to discuss—"

"It was something I had always wanted to try," she went on, standing to stack the dirty dishes on the table. "It wasn't really a dangerous climb, and it was so beautiful that summer. Of course, when your father and I got engaged, the trip was out of the question. It was important that we save every penny, and Carl was concerned about the risks involved. He said he would be worried sick."

My mother the nutritionist—climbing mountains in Wyoming? The thought fairly boggled my mind. Automatically I began to help her clear the table, my thoughts going a hundred miles an hour. "Did you ever climb it?" I asked. "The Grand Teton?"

She smiled and shook her head. "No, I'm afraid not. Opportunities like that only come along once in a lifetime."

My father stood up stiffly, as if he had hurt his back. "Irene, I never insisted that you stay home from that expedition."

She kissed him on the cheek, being careful not to soil his white shirt with the dirty plates she carried. "Of course you didn't. And I never insisted that I go." She flashed me a smile, looking far younger than her thirty-nine years.

"Chelsea, love, you're going to need a sleeping bag. Maybe Sandy's parents will lend us one."

Long after everyone else was asleep that night, I sat in a tiny little ball on my window seat, watching the mist floating in and around and behind a three-quarter moon. I searched the sky—unsuccessfully—for the Big Dipper and the North Star. Ranger would know where to find all of the constellations. He seemed to know everything and anything about the great outdoors. Chelsea Anne Hyatt, late-blooming feminist, knew nothing.

A five-day river trip would probably kill me.

I faced the inescapable truth. My brief moment of glory at the dinner table had landed me in an unholy mess. Pride would not let me back down, and common sense told me that I wouldn't live to see my senior year.

Jess Calahan. The name suddenly flashed in my mind like a neon sign. Jess . . . probably short for Jesse. No doubt he was named after some wretched mountain man. If it were not for Jess Calahan, I would be peacefully asleep at this very moment.

Suddenly I wanted to see this faceless person who had turned my life upside down. I made my way carefully across the room and clicked on the small decorative lamp beside my bed. Soft pink light filtered through the shade, barely reaching to the corner bookcase. My high school yearbook occupied a place of honor on the center shelf. I took it back to bed with me and turned to the section with pictures of last year's graduating glass. Cabot, Cahoon, Calahan . . . Jess Calahan.

Like all yearbook pictures since time began, it was fuzzy around the edges and slightly underdeveloped. Only Jess Calahan's eyes seemed to have any clarity about them. They were deep-set and heavy-lidded, almost sleepy-looking. By some miracle the photographer had failed to color them the same startling orange that transformed the other students on the page into glowing-eyed aliens. Jess's eyes were the most amazing shade of golden-brown that I had ever seen.

The eyes of a madman, I decided bitterly.

I slammed the yearbook closed and let it drop to the floor.

Chapter 2

I thought about writing a will.

Sitting on a rolled-up sleeping bag in the middle of a parking lot at five o'clock in the morning, there was little else to do. We weren't due to gather at the offices of Calahan Expeditions until five-thirty. Thanks to Ranger Rick's fear that we might be caught in a traffic jam (such a common occurrence at that hour), my bleary-eyed father had dropped us off at the midtown office building thirty minutes ahead of schedule. For the first time in my life I was up and dressed before the moon had disappeared from the sky. I watched the street-cleaning crews at work, waved to a solitary jogger, and witnessed firsthand the streetlights going out one by one. The excitement nearly killed me.

Ranger and Sandy sat together on his duffel bag. Sandy was listening with a rapt expression while Ranger explained the finer details of constructing a rabbit snare. Either my poor, deluded friend had developed a sudden passion for hunting furry animals or she was a better actress than I'd thought. Either way, I had the sinking feeling that I would be spending the next five days as a third wheel. Provided I survived that long.

I rummaged quickly through my industrial-size purse, searching for a scrap of paper on which to record my Last Will and Testament. Before I found an old envelope I had emptied the contents of my bag in front of me on the asphalt.

"What the devil . . ." Ranger's mouth was literally hanging open. He stared at the clutter and slowly shook his head from side to side. "I don't believe it. What did you bring all that garbage for? Look at it!"

I looked. I saw my manicure kit, my embroidered make-up bag, perfume, deodorant, hair spray, a small freezer bag stuffed with foam-rubber curlers, and a bottle of sunscreen. There were also several incidentals such as dental floss, breath mints, hand lotion, Chapstick, and so on. Nothing I saw even remotely resembled garbage.

"So what?" I covered my mouth to stifle a yawn. "You told me to bring the bare necessities."

"I meant your clothes, airhead! You're not going to need any of that junk on a river trip. Where do you think we're going, to some kind of fashion show?"

"That's the trouble with camping." I smiled sweetly. "It has a bad reputation because everyone goes around looking like they just crawled out from under a rock."

Ranger rolled his eyes in disgust. "Is that so? I suppose I should be grateful you didn't bring bubble bath to make the river all pink and sweet-smelling. You know, you ought to take a few lessons from Sandy. You don't see her carrying all that stuff."

Loyalty to my best friend kept me silent. True, she had brought along only one bulging duffel bag, but I knew very well that everything but the kitchen sink had been crammed into it, including a battery-operated Water-Pic. Sandy caught my eyes and smiled weakly, tightening the drawstrings on her duffel bag.

A metal-gray van pulling a small trailer turned into the parking lot, sparing me any further lectures. The words

CALAHAN EXPEDITIONS were neatly lettered on the side of the van. Our transportation to the River of No Return had arrived.

Ranger jumped to his feet, nearly knocking Sandy off the duffel bag in his excitement. Two people emerged from the van. One was a heavyset man of about fifty; the other was a tall, broad-shouldered boy with sun-streaked blond hair and an easy smile. I recognized Jess Calahan immediately.

I watched him walk toward us with a sudden dryness in my throat. In all honesty I had to admit that his picture didn't do him justice. He looked as if he lived in the sun. His skin was the color of polished teak, a startling contrast to the white "Calahan Expeditions" T-shirt he wore. His hair was longer than the current style, brushed carelessly back from his face. His sleepy-looking burned-honey eyes gleamed with laughter as he responded to something Ranger said. From a purely clinical standpoint I decided that the outdoors type did have a certain appeal.

While I scrambled to gather up the contents of my purse, Ranger introduced Sandy to Jess Calahan. Then he motioned to where I squatted on the ground, adding carelessly, "That's my sister, Chelsea. This will be the first time she's slept apart from her electric blanket, Lord help us all."

Jess smiled and held out a hand to help me to my feet. His expression held a casual friendliness and something else, a kind of amused curiosity. "You're in for a treat, then," he said politely. "The Colorado is beautiful this time of year."

I met Ranger's eyes defiantly over Jess Calahan's shoulder. "I can hardly wait."

The van driver had been busy checking the contents of the trailer. Now he ambled toward us, moving like a sleepy bear who had just come out of hibernation. He wore baggy jeans, a brilliant Hawaiian shirt, and a baseball cap with a

Mickey Mouse emblem stitched on the front. He was even more deeply tanned than Jess, and his face was lined and creased like a particularly difficult jigsaw puzzle. A day's growth of beard added to his swarthy complexion, making him look like an old pirate with a campy sense of fashion.

"My uncle, Mike Calahan," Jess said. "Mike took me on my first river trip about the same time I learned to walk. Mike, I'd like you to meet Ranger Hyatt, his sister, Chelsea, and Sandy DeSpain."

Mr. Calahan shook Ranger's hand with such force that my brother's cheeks actually vibrated. Then he swung on me and I jumped, clasping my hands behind my back. I had not spent twenty dollars on artificial nails just to have them ground to dust in a thirty-second handshake.

"So you want to be a river rat?" Mr. Calahan barked.

I wasn't sure whether to laugh or be insulted. "I beg your pardon?"

"A river rat." Jess grinned. "Anyone who makes it home from five days on the Colorado is an official river rat."

"Have there been many?" I asked faintly. "That didn't make it back, I mean?"

"Quite a few, come to think of it." Mr. Calahan frowned, folding his arms across a massive chest. "'Course, they were girls mostly. We just threw them overboard. Fish food."

I managed a sickly smile. "The man is kidding," I whispered to Sandy. "Isn't he?"

Sandy shrugged helplessly, looking a little green around the edges.

The parking lot came alive within the next five minutes. Several cars arrived, and Jess and Ranger kept busy loading everyone's gear into the trailer. After a while I noticed with surprise that all the potential river rats scurrying around bidding good-bye to their sleepy parents were dressed identically. Each wore blue shorts and a blue short-sleeved shirt with a gold scarf around the neck. Not one was over twelve years old.

The light dawned—painfully.

I walked slowly to the trailer, watching as Ranger and Jess made a pyramid of army-green duffel bags. If looks could kill, I would have been an only child from that moment on.

"Ranger?" I called sweetly, trying not to gag. "Could I talk to you for a minute?"

He jumped down from the trailer, wiping his forehead with his shirttail. "What's up?"

"Why didn't you tell me?" I asked in a fierce whisper.

Ranger blinked wide gray eyes. I could tell he was enjoying himself immensely. "Tell you what, sis?"

"Boy Scouts!" I snapped, forgetting to keep my voice down. "We're going on this trip with a whole herd of Boy Scouts!"

"Not a herd," he corrected calmly. "A troop. Seven, to be exact. It just looks like more when they're running around like this. Count them when they slow down."

"I'll get you for this," I promised him darkly. "Somehow, someday, when you are least expecting it—"

"Miss Hyatt!"

This time Michael Calahan's earsplitting voice startled me into swallowing my chewing gum. I whirled to face him, struggling for air.

He carried my duffel bag in one hand, my overnight case in the other. "Is this your gear?"

I nodded. Now what?

"One bag," he said. "Each person is allowed one duffel bag. You've booked passage on a six-man raft, Hyatt, not the *Loveboat*. I'll store this extra bag in the office here till we get back."

"Hold it!" I managed to transfer my shampoo and toothbrush to the duffel bag before Mr. Calahan shuffled off toward the office with the overnight case. I distinctly heard him mutter something about little ladies sticking to their knitting.

"Don't mind him," Jess advised from behind me. "Mike Calahan is the last of the world's great chauvinists. He still thinks the biggest mistake this country ever made was giving women the vote."

I think I was suffering from shock at having been separated from my makeup kit. When I turned on Jess, the blood was boiling in my cheeks. "And what about you?" I shot back. "Does it bother you to have girls along on river trips?"

A smile gleamed in Jess's golden eyes as he considered the question. "We took a group of senior citizens down the Colorado last week," he said thoughtfully. "Five men and two very spirited ladies. Everyone had a great time, even Mike. No, I can honestly say that it has never bothered me to have females along on a river run . . . until now."

I didn't miss the slight emphasis on the last two words. "Until now," I repeated pointedly. "Terrific. Senior citizens and Boy Scouts qualify, but teenage girls are a handicap. That's discrimination, you know."

"Not exactly. You asked me if it bothered me to have girls along. It never has." He raised his hand, flicking me lightly on the nose with a calloused brown finger. "But then, I've never had anyone along who looked like you."

I searched my brain for a snappy comeback, but my mind was working like cold oatmeal. There is nothing worse than being angry with someone and having him throw a compliment in your face.

Jess nudged the duffel bag at my feet with his shoe. "Load your gear, Hyatt," he said solemnly. "I'd offer to do it for you, but I know how you liberated types feel about these things."

Living all my life in the shadow of the Rocky Mountains

had not prepared me for a close encounter with the real thing.

It was incredible. Monster mountains loomed on either side of the van, leaving just enough room for a twisting two-lane strip of asphalt and a swollen, roaring river, the very same river I would soon be bobbing up and down on in a little rubber boat.

For the hundredth time I looked out my window at the brown, swirling water crashing against the cliffbanks so dangerously close to the road. This did not fit my image of a river at all. A river was blue and clear and flowed gently over smooth white pebbles. A river was not wild and mud-colored and filled with rotting leaves and broken limbs. This river looked downright sinister.

"Relax, will you?"

I turned to Ranger, forcing a hollow smile. "Oh, I'm relaxed. Really. It's amazing how close Mr. Calahan can drive to the edge of the road without falling into the river, don't you think?"

My artificial enthusiasm fell flat. Ranger grinned and patted me gently on the shoulder. "Keep the faith, Chelsea. Mike Calahan could probably drive this road with his eyes closed. Jess told me they've taken more than fifteen trips down the Colorado and Yampa rivers this summer alone."

As far as I was concerned, this only proved that Calahan and Jess both had a death wish, but I didn't say so. "All the same, I'll be glad when we get off this road."

Ranger nodded fervently, his eyes taking on the glazed sheen of a religious fanatic. "I know what you mean. Once we get to Reardon's Pass, all we have to do is inflate the boats and we're on our way. I've been looking forward to this for months."

All the squirrels were not in the woods. I turned my head toward the window to hide a smile. I caught sight of a lone fisherman in hip boots standing at the edge of the boiling water. "Why do we have to drive all the way to Reardon's Pass when we've been following the river for more than an hour?"

"We can't put in along here," Ranger replied, proudly displaying his superior knowledge. "It's too rough and too deep. There's a ramp at Reardon's Pass that was built just to accommodate rafts. The water is calm there, and you have time for a few lessons on river running before you hit the first rapids."

Ranger continued to lecture me on the basics of water survival while I sat very still in the corner of the seat and tried not to be carsick. It was a twelve-passenger van with four rows of black vinyl benches. Somehow Sandy had ended up in the front of the car between Mike and Jess Calahan. A sea of Boy Scouts separated us. Each kid possessed a year's supply of bubble gum (already chewed and stored in their freckled cheeks) and an endless stream of knock-knock jokes. Ranger and I were seated in the back of the van with a fragile-looking kid, whose scout shorts hung way past his knobby little knees. He had told us his name was Cameron Jones, and he shook Ranger's hand with solemn dignity. Ranger had spent the better part of the drive teaching him to play poker, an achievement I was sure Cameron's mother would be thrilled about.

My stomach began to roll and sway with every switch-back on the winding canyon road. I looked up at Sandy to see how she was faring. She was laughing at something Jess had said, leaning her head back so that her hair brushed the arm he rested casually on the back of the seat. If she was nauseous, she certainly hid it well. If it bothered her to have the river lapping at the road, she didn't show it. She looked perfectly calm and relaxed, and I had a sudden urge to borrow Cameron's peashooter and let her have it with one of the spit-wads he was spraying around the van. After all, she had been the one with the bright idea of following her heart down the Colorado River. I was only here because I was such a loyal and devoted friend. The least Sandy could have done was sit in the back of the van and get carsick with me.

Catty. I was being catty, and it wasn't my style. I was here because I had let Ranger and my father goad me into it. My stomach was affecting my disposition, and if I didn't get my feet onto solid ground, my stomach would affect the floor of the van.

Ranger nudged me and asked if I wanted a Reese's Peanut Butter Cup. I clamped my hand over my mouth and closed my eyes, tasting the orange juice I'd had for breakfast.

Reardon Pass appeared just in time. It was a one-street town nestled at the base of a rugged-looking mountain. I scrambled out of the van the moment it stopped and started gulping deep breaths of pine-scented air, heavily spiced with the unmistakable aroma of fish. The river rumbled in the background, out of sight but obviously nearby.

We were parked in front of a small A-frame building tucked in a stand of straggly-looking pines. A hand-painted sign in the window declared it to be the REARDON PASS CAFÉ, LAST HOT FOOD FOR TWENTY MILES. A smaller sign offered, PLUMP NIGHTCRAWLERS, 75¢ A DOZEN. I nearly lost it right there in the parking lot before I realized that the worms were sold to fishermen as bait and not as the special of the day.

Boy Scouts were scuttling around me like busy little ants. They all seemed to know exactly what they were doing. Sandy and I followed their example and pulled our duffel bags out of the trailer, trudging after the boys in blue down a narrow dirt track that led behind the café.

I practically fell into the Colorado River. In the few minutes since I had last seen it, the river had been transformed from a raging maelstrom into a kiddie wadding pool. It lapped gently on the sandy shore, sparkling blue-white diamonds in the sunlight. I could still hear the ominous roaring of an angry river, yet as far as I could see, the Colorado was beautifully, peacefully calm. It isn't me making that awful racket, it seemed to say, I must be some other river.

I didn't trust it.

All too soon Mike Calahan had backed his trailer down to the water, and the rest of the supplies were unloaded. Two large black bundles of canvas and rubber grew magically into rafts with the help of a gas cylinder. They were far larger than I had imagined, easily big enough for seven or eight passengers. Sausagelike pontoons ballooned along the edges of the flat-bottomed boats, meeting at the front and back in a puffy *V* shape that resembled the prow of a ship. Duffel bags and provisions were lashed into the center of the rafts with ropes, and fluorescent-orange life jackets were passed around. I strapped mine on so tightly, my ribs began to hurt.

Jess double-checked Sandy's vest, then mine. "Chelsea, can you breathe?"

I gasped for air. "Certainly. Hey! Don't take it off! I'm a lousy swimmer."

"I'm not taking it off," he reassured me. "I'm loosening the straps. Believe me, being strangled by a life jacket is a nasty way to go."

"Drowning isn't any picnic, either," I mumbled.

He glanced up at me, then back to the strap he was refastening beneath my chin. "Can I ask you something?"

Now and then his finger brushed the skin at the base of my throat. His wide shoulders blocked the sunlight, and I shivered, but not because I was cold. I bent my head and focused on the waterproof diver's watch he wore. "Sure. Ask away."

"What are you doing here?"

His question took me by surprise. "Doing here? I'm doing what everyone else is—going on a river trip."

He shook his head, giving the strap one final tug. "Nope. I can't see it."

I tried to look at the knot beneath my chin. Did I have a defective life jacket? "Can't see what?"

"You." He stepped backward, and the sunlight washed over me. I winced at the flaming red sunspots exploding behind my eyes. "I can't see you as a river rat," he went on thoughtfully, stuffing his hands in the pockets of his jeans. "You just aren't the type. The thing I can't figure out is why the devil you signed up in the first place. It's pretty obvious that you would rather walk barefoot over hot coals then get into one of these boats."

He was irritating me again. Jess Calahan had a positive gift for it. It made no difference that he had hit the nail right on the head. I was fairly certain that the next five days would kill me, but I wasn't about to admit this to him.

"I'm beginning to think Mike Calahan isn't the only chauvinist in your family," I said coolly. "I suppose you think Sandy doesn't belong on a river trip, either?"

"Oh, Sandy will do fine," he replied. "She's a rookie, but she seems like she has a level head on her shoulders. I don't think she's the type to burst into tears if she gets her hair wet."

I clenched my teeth. "And I am, I suppose?"

"I didn't say that." He grinned. "No, I do not think you're the type to cry over wet hair."

"Then what type am I?" I persisted, itching for a fight.

"Well . . ." He paused to consider. "I sure as heck can't see you building lean-tos and emptying Porta-Potties. No, I think you're more the homecoming princess type. You know, the girl in the long pink dress who rides in a Cadillac convertible around the football field at halftime. Five-foot-two, eyes of blue, and dates the captain of the football team."

I gaped at him. "That was almost a year ago. How did you remember the color of my dress?"

"You're kidding!" Jess threw back his head, and the laughter gleamed in his sunlit eyes. "You mean you really *were* homecoming princess last year?"

"You went to Skyview too," I said stiffly. "I thought you had remembered."

"I guess I never paid too much attention to that kind of thing. I'm a better judge of women than I thought. How did I do on the rest of it? Are you going with the captain of the football team?"

Stubbornly I kept silent. So I had gone out with Gary Quinn a few times. I certainly wouldn't call it "going" with him.

"Jess! Get a move on! We're wasting daylight."

It was Mike Calahan, his voice oddly distant. I turned, surprised to see one of the rafts arleady floating away from shore. I could make out Sandy's bright yellow sweatshirt and Ranger's battered cowboy hat with the colorful feathered band. Excited Boy Scouts clambered back and forth across the mound of supplies in the center of the boat.

And in the other raft, still resting on the sand, Cameron Jones and three of his bubble-blowing buddies were waiting with thinly disguised impatience.

"Time to go," Jess said cheerfully. "Any last words, princess?"

"Yes." I smiled sweetly. "What are we waiting for?"

We paddled away from shore until the current caught our boat, carrying us steadily down the middle of the river. Trees slipped rapidly by, growing in the most grotesque positions from sheer, jagged rock. Now and again the shoreline reverted to gently wooded slopes. Then the sun's warmth would disappear, and we would float through the shadows of colorless sandstone cliffs that were hundreds of feet high.

Once on the water, Jess Calahan's teasing attitude vanished completely. He was thoroughly professional, giving us instructions on a steady, patient drone for half an hour. We were told what to do in an emergency, how to safely maneuver our boat through rapids, and when and how to use the paddles to guide us to shore. I clung fiercely to the rope that secured the supplies and tried to concentrate on Jess's words, but it was easier said than done. The floor of the boat was cold and kept heaving and lurching beneath me. A fine spray came over the rim, wetting my face and hair. In the distance I could see Mike Calahan's boat, bobbing up and down like a CrackerJack toy. I wondered if Sandy felt as lost as I did.

For the first time in my life there wasn't a 7-11 store in sight. I was completely out of touch with civilization.

" . . . but it's nothing to worry about," Jess was saying. "The river takes everybody by surprise sooner or later. The main thing is not to panic. If you fall overboard, your life jacket will keep you up. Keep an eye out for rocks and enjoy your swim till we pull you in. I can gaurantee that each and every one of you will either fall in"—he grinned —"or be pushed out before this trip is over. Until then you're not a genuine river rat."

My knees were cramped from sitting so rigidly. I shifted my position, leaning back against the pontoon. For one moment I released my stranglehold on the rope and flexed my numbed fingers. A red welt slashed diagonally across my palm.

This was ridiculous. Boy Scouts frolicked around the raft like it was a jungle gym, while I sat paralyzed with fear. What was there to be afraid of, anyway? So I happened to be floating down a river. The current was perfectly calm and sluggish at the moment. This was no different than floating on my air mattress at the Rec Center pool.

Carefully I levered myself to a sitting position on the pontoon. The air was warm against my face, smelling more of damp earth than of fish. I could feel the sun heating the center part of my hair, relaxing the muscles that had knotted in my neck.

I smiled at my fears, feeling the tension drain out of my body. This wasn't bad at all.

Suddenly the boat seemed to buckle, pitching me upward. I saw whirling trees and mountains before I went head first into the cold, murky water. I came up sputtering, swallowing a mouthful of the Colorado. Hair and water blinded my eyes, and my ears were gurgling like a spring.

The current pulled at my legs, but my life jacket kept me bouncing like a beach ball on top of the water. I groped wildly for a handhold as I tossed against the side of the raft. Strong hands grabbed my arms, and slimy, cold rubber brushed my face.

"Up and go, Chelsea. One, two . . . three."

"Three" landed me face first in the bottom of the raft. Using the last of my pitiful reserves of strength, I rolled over and leaned my head weakly against a duffel bag.

Four little scout faces were peering over me. One of them broke into giggles, starting a chain reaction. The kids fell backward over the supplies, holding their sides and kicking their skinny legs in the air.

Jess pushed a towel into my face. "Congratulations, Crewman Hyatt. You are our first official river rat. You don't believe in wasting any time, do you?"

I glared at him, wiping the clinging strands of hair from my face. "Why didn't you warn me?"

He looked puzzled and more than a little amused. "Warn you about what?"

"The rapids! Why didn't you tell me they were coming

up? If I'd had a little warning, I might have been able to hold on!''

He blinked at me, then burst out laughing. ''Chelsea, if we had run into rapids, you would have known three miles in advance. You hear a rumbling that gets louder and louder until it sounds like Niagara Falls. This portion of the river is as calm as a summer's day. We won't see any white water until tomorrow.''

I was bewildered. ''Then what happened?''

''The boat glanced off a boulder. It happens all the time. It's one of the things you have to watch out for if you don't want to spend most of your time in the drink.''

Reminding myself that I was not the kind of girl to cry over wet hair, I rubbed my eyes with my fists. My hands came away black.

''Do I have mascara all over my face?'' I asked quietly.

''Yeah.'' Jess grinned. ''You look like a modern oil painting.''

I covered my head with the towel and curled into a wet, miserable ball. Lesson number one. Never confuse the Colorado with a swimming pool. It may be the last thing you ever do.

Chapter 3

The flickering firelight cast trembling shadows on the water-packed sand. I sat on an uncomfortable log, hugging my knees to keep warm. Beside me Sandy held her hands out to the fire, her face reflecting its shimmering orange glow. Her nose and cheeks were flushed with color from a day on the water, and a contented smile curved her lips.

"Isn't this terrific?" she asked. "I'm really beginning to see why Ranger loves the mountains so much. Smell this air! Did you notice how much better food tastes when it's cooked outdoors? Those hamburgers tasted like steak! And just look at that sky, Chelsea. I've never seen so many stars in my life. It's like black velvet sprinkled with diamonds."

"Don't get poetic on me," I warned, burrowing my chin into the collar of my parka. "I'm not in the mood. Do you think we could move this log a little closer to the fire?"

"Not without setting ourselves aflame," Sandy replied wryly. "You'd think that you'd be able to keep warm with two sweaters and a coat. It just isn't that cold tonight."

"My bones have been frozen since I fell into the river this afternoon. I can't warm up. Even my teeth are cold."

"Move around," Sandy advised. "Walk up and down the beach a few times and get your blood circulating."

I shook my head emphatically. "Oh, no. At least here by the fire I can see any vicious furries creeping up on me. I'm not going to take the chance of having a close encounter with a bear or something."

"There aren't any bears around here." Sandy twisted on the log and tried to peer into the darkness behind us. "I mean, surely someone would have warned us if there were bears—right?"

I shrugged, thinking of the towering sandstone cliff that backed our small campground. It was pitted with caves and tunnels that looked perfect for housing bears and the like. "The only thing we are definitely safe from in this wilderness is a traffic accident. And muggers. There probably aren't many of them in the mountains."

"What's that about muggers?" Ranger asked, entering the circle of light with an armful of wood.

"Just counting my blessings," I muttered, watching him feed the popping fire. On the other side of the flames Mike Calahan sat with seven wide-eyed scouts, telling them ghost stories in a deep, gravelly voice. Now and again I caught such phrases as "beady, glowing eyes" and "the silent specter from the river bottom." My goose bumps began to get goose bumps.

Somewhere up in the black hillside a stealthy rustling broke the silence. I strained to hear over Rangers' and Sandy's chatter. The sound came again, much closer this time.

"There's something out there," I blurted. "Listen . . . Ranger, will you shut up and listen? There!" It came again, like furtive footsteps moving toward the camp. "Did you hear it?"

"I heard it," Ranger replied calmly. "Could be anything. Coyote, cougar, maybe a mountain lion. It has to be of pretty good size to make that much noise."

My hand grabbed Sandy's arm convulsively. A light broke through the woods, milky-white and darting back and forth over the ground. Jess followed behind, carrying a flashlight and a small ax.

"I was right," Ranger said. "He is big. Six feet, at least."

Jess laughed, clicking off the flashlight and squatting beside me. "Are you trying to put a scare into the girls? Ranger, you belong over there with the scouts. They love a good horror story."

Ranger threw me a self-satisfied grin. "Oh, I don't know. I've got a pretty gullible audience right here."

"Remind me to push you out of the boat tomorrow," Sandy said. "About the time we hit the rapids."

The rapids. I relived the sensation of cold, swirling waters closing over my head, filling my nose and mouth. Jess had compared tomorrow's rapids with Niagara Falls. Exaggeration or not, it was a comparison I could have done without.

"It wouldn't do any good," I said to Sandy, doing my best to disguise the tremors in my voice. "He would float, even without his life jacket. It's all that hot air—"

"Speaking of floating," Ranger interrupted neatly, "I heard you took a little dip yourself this afternoon. How was the water, sis?"

"Wet," I said shortly.

"Too bad." He grinned, obviously delighted. "You know, I have to hand it to you, Chelsea. I never thought you would actually get in one of those boats, let alone survive a dunking. I'm seeing a side of you I've never seen before—stringy hair, no makeup, mosquito bites all over your face. It makes me wish I had a camera. I'd love to take a picture of you and show it to Gary Quinn when we get back. I'll bet he wouldn't come around half so often."

What had I ever done to deserve such a charming brother? In the firelight I could see Jess watching me carefully, a smile playing around the edges of his mouth. "This Gary Quinn," he said to Ranger. "He wouldn't be a football player, by any chance?"

"Captain of the team." Ranger nodded glumly. "He drives a black Trans-Am with this cross-eyed eagle painted all over the hood. His dad bought it for him when Skyview won the state championship last year. Sort of a twenty-thousand-dollar pat on the back."

Beside me, so softly that only I could hear, Jess murmured. "Boy, did I have you pegged, princess."

"I'll never understand what girls see in those rich, preppy types," my brother the motor mouth went on. "Other than money, looks, and popularity, the poor buggers haven't got a thing going for them."

Jess smiled absently, but said nothing. He picked up a piece of bark in the sand and tossed it into the fire. Sparks popped and spiraled wildly into the sky above us, glowing brilliantly for a few brief seconds.

"Did you hear that?" Roger said suddenly. "A screech owl, just in those pines behind Mike. C'mon Jess, let's take a look."

"You take a look," Jess said lazily. "Take the flashlight. I'm too comfortable to even think about getting up again. Maybe Sandy would like to see one."

Sandy hesitated. "Do they bite?"

Ranger pulled her off the log impatiently. "No, they don't bite. And it's very seldom that you're going to get a chance to see a screech owl in its natural habitat. You are in for a real treat, girl."

"Aaah." Sandy nodded, throwing me a wry look over her shoulder. "I'm in for a treat, Chelsea. Did you hear that?"

After Ranger and Sandy had gone, the silence stretched and became awkward. Normally I had no trouble making conversation with boys, but normally I didn't look like Frankenstein's bride. My hair had frizzled into a dirty-blond horse's mane, and my skin was coated with a fine dusting of river silt. My clothes had dried into something resembling stiff burlap, and I smelled like a half-baked trout. I had no fears of Ranger showing Gary Quinn my photograph. He would never in a million years recognize the girl he called "Angel Face."

Finally I said the first thing that came to mind. "It's a beautiful night."

Jess's mouth quirked. "Beautiful," he agreed. "Tell me, do you always shiver like that on beautiful nights?"

I clenched my teeth to keep them from clacking together. "I can't help it. I'm a little . . . cold."

"Why didn't you say so?" Jess stood, shrugged out of his windbreaker, and dropped it over my shoulders. "This jacket is better than a parka. The lining is sheepskin."

"I can't take your coat," I protested. "You'll freeze. I was lying when I said it was a beautiful night. I think my nose is getting frostbite, and I have two blocks of ice where my feet used to be."

He laughed and knelt down by the fire, looking perfectly comfortable in a lightweight plaid shirt. "It's that dunking you took today. The water's pretty cold if you aren't used to it. It takes awhile to warm up again."

"I don't see how anybody ever gets used to this," I muttered, slapping a mosquito that was feasting on my cheek. "It would be like getting used to the flu."

Jess poked a twig into the fire until the end began to glow. "I guess it depends on how you look at it," he said quietly. "Uncle Mike helped me to appreciate the wilderness areas. He made me realize how few people ever get to see things like a deer with a day-old fawn or an eagle soaring in the sky. I know I sound like I'm standing on a soapbox, but I feel pretty lucky to have had those experiences."

"You're always talking about Mike," I said curiously. "I thought your father owned Calahan Expeditions?"

"He did." Jess brought the burning stick close to his face and stared into my eyes over the flame. "He and Mike ran it together for the first few years. Neither one of them were educated men. They started Calahan Expeditions because it seemed like a good way to combine their knowledge of the outdoors with making a living. They never got rich, but it didn't matter. They were doing what they loved. Not many people can afford to do that these days."

I thought of my own father and the time he spent away from home, sleeping in commercial airliners and eating alone in strange cities. I knew he was proud of his reputation and of the material things he was able to provide us with, but I had never heard him say whether he actually enjoyed his work. And I had never thought to ask.

"Your father . . ." I said hesitantly. "You said he and Mike used to run the business?"

Jess dropped the twig to the sand as the orange-tipped flame reached his fingers. "In the beginning. My dad was killed in a freeway accident when I was six. It's kind of ironic. He hated freeways, almost never drove on them. I guess it came from spending so much time in the mountains." He smiled sadly. "You don't run into too much traffic up here, even at five o'clock. Anyway, Mike's been kind of a surrogate father to me since then."

"I'm sorry." Inadequate, but I didn't know what else to say. I couldn't imagine growing up without a father. Despite my own father's extensive traveling, he had always managed to be there for Ranger and me when we needed him. And whenever he was gone, he never went a day without talking to each of us on the phone. I realized with a kind of shock that I had always taken that kind of security for granted.

"Don't be. It was a long time ago." Jess stood up and stretched in the flickering light. "I think I'll go round up the two owl-watchers. It's about time everyone turned in.

We'll need to get an early start in the morning if we're going to make it to Chicken Cliff before nightfall.''

"Chicken Cliff?" I got to my feet, hating the sandy grit that filled my shoes. "What's that?"

Jess grinned and disappeared into the shadows. His voice floated back to me, disembodied. "It's a surprise, princess.''

A mound of sand hit me between the shoulders. Another pushed up beneath my left hip. My head rested lower than my feet, and when I reversed my sleeping bag, a whole new set of humps rose up to greet me.

I tried counting sheep, but they quickly turned into bears. I tossed and turned until I was a prisoner in a down-filled pretzel. I fought my way free, unzipped the bag, smoothed it out, and zipped myself in again. A screech owl signaled the beginning of round two.

Through it all Sandy slept like a baby. She had returned from her walk with Ranger unusually quiet. I had expected her to fill me in on her latest efforts to captivate my brother, but she merely smiled and gave me an absent-minded good night before crawling into her sleeping bag. Less than a minute later I heard the tiny, breathless snores that had driven me crazy at slumber parties since I was ten years old.

The whispers and giggles of the scouts sleeping along the sandy shoreline finally settled into silence. Ranger and Jess were talking quietly beside the spent fire, and Mike Calahan had disappeared, head and all, into a blue-and-white-plaid sleeping bag. I had no idea what time it was. My watch was at the bottom of the Colorado. It could have been midnight or close to dawn or not yet time for the nine o'clock news.

I rolled over to escape a rock, and the bag rolled with me. I had to stifle an urge to scream and kick at the wretched thing until I was free.

"Chelsea?"

The faint voice nearly sent me to the tops of the pine trees. I pushed myself up on my elbows and stared at the forlorn figure before me. Rumpled hair, pale face, knobby little knees. A sleeping bag dragged behind him.

"Cameron?" I whispered. "What are you doing up? You should have been asleep hours ago."

He shrugged, swiping at his nose with one hand. "Those guys rolled their sleeping bags out too close to the water. The sand's sort of wet, you know?"

He shifted his weight awkwardly from one foot to the other, as if he didn't know whether to stay or go. I recalled Mike Calahan's ghost stories and had to hide a smile. Maybe the "silent specter from the river bottom" had been a bit too much for poor old Cameron.

"I know what you mean," I said wisely. "There's nothing worse than rolling your sleeping bag out on wet sand. Why don't you sleep up here with us?"

I didn't have to ask twice. Within seconds Cameron was snuggled in his mummy-style sleeping bag, the drawstring pulled tight until nothing but his nose and mouth could be seen. "I can't wait till tomorrow," he said. "Those rapids are really supposed to be something. Jess says it's like taking the wildest roller-coaster ride in the whole world. You ever been to Disneyland?"

"Two years ago." I swatted at something white fluttering over my nose.

"Did you go on Space Mountain?"

"Nope. But Ranger did. He threw up."

"I went on it seven times," he said proudly. "I never got sick. I would have gone on it some more, but I ran out of tickets."

I sighed, looking through tangled pine boughs at the sky. I had never dreamed that stars could look so close. "You know, Cameron," I said softly, "there's one big difference between the rides at Disneyland and the

Colorado River. They strap you into all those rides at Disneyland so you can't fall out. But when we hit the rapids"—I shivered—"there's nothing to keep us in the raft. After one drenching today, I'm not really excited about going under again tomorrow. You know what I mean, Bud?"

Had Sandy suddenly started snoring in double time? "Cameron? Hey, are you asleep?"

There was no answer. The snug little sleeping bag rose and fell with deep, even breathing.

"Some friend you are," I muttered beneath my breath. "Leaving me alone to fight off the silent specter! What do you care if my feet are frozen and my sleeping bag is lumpy and I can't get Jess Calahan out of my mind?" There. I'd finally said it, if only to a sleeping Boy Scout. "I know . . . it's crazy. The river rat and the cream puff. Wouldn't Ranger get a kick out of that one?"

Cameron groaned and rolled over. Even in his sleep I was boring him.

"Sweet dreams, scout," I whispered. I wriggled and squirmed in my sleeping bag until I was only moderately uncomfortable. I began counting stars. I was still counting when an apricot sun rose over the eastern ridge.

Chapter 4

"Waltzin' Matilda, waltzin' Matilda . . ."

Singing. Someone—or something—was singing. I shifted miserably in my sleeping bag, feeling a thousand cramped muscles scream in protest. Who could possibly be so rude as to sing at the top of their lungs first thing in the morning? Didn't he know I had been awake the entire blessed night?

The singing stopped. I was almost asleep again when the harmonica playing began.

Sandy emerged from her sleeping bag, one eye open and the other shut. "What's that? That awful noise . . . what is it?"

"Bad dreams," I mumbled. "Bad, bad dreams. Go back to sleep."

But there was no sleep to be had. The cliffs echoed with a tinny rendition of "She'll Be Coming 'Round the Mountain," followed by the mournful strains of "Shenandoah." Finally Sandy and I both gave up the fight, crawling out of our bags and blinking in the harsh, white sunlight.

The camp was slowly coming alive. Rumpled-looking

scouts knelt at the river's edge, splashing their faces with ice-cold water. Jess and Ranger sat on a log near the camp fire, each holding a paper plate. And Mike Calahan, resplendent in a lemon-yellow football jersey and matching headband, sat nearby in a folding camp chair. There was a small silver harmonica gleaming where his mouth should have been.

Sandy spoke softly out of the side of her mouth. "Do you remember when Blake Dobbs played his accordian in the school assembly and I said it was the worst thing I'd ever heard?"

"Uh-huh."

"I take it back."

Mike spotted us and the music ceased abruptly. "It's about time," he bellowed. "Load your gear and grab a bite. This is no drill. It's the real thing!"

Jess caught my eye and grinned. "Translation," he said. "Uncle Mike says good morning, and he hopes you slept well. If you would like some breakfast, the pancakes are ready."

The shock of seeing those golden-brown eyes had the same effect on me as a sudden plunge into the Colorado. I was wide-awake, from the top of my matted hair to the toes of my dirty socks. I felt positively *Neanderthal*.

I smiled, feeling my chapped lips crack. Grabbing Sandy's hand, I walked backward toward our duffel bags. "We'll be ready," I promised faintly. "Just give us a minute."

A minute turned into twenty as Sandy and I made a necessary trip into the trees and another down to the river to wash. After changing into a clean pair of shorts and a pale blue top that matched my eyes, I felt almost human again. Hadn't I read that the natural look was "in" this year? What could be more natural than a sunburned nose and mosquito bites?

While Mike provided mood music, Jess dished out buckwheat pancakes on Styrofoam plates. I found myself a one-passenger log near the river's edge, hidden from the camp by a grove of cottonwood trees. The river seemed higher than yesterday, churning a bubbling foam over partially submerged boulders. A blackened tree limb floated by, turning slow-motion circles in the steady current. The water should have taken on some sort of color in the clear morning light, yet it stubbornly retained the appearance of dirty dishwater.

I ate slowly, obeying for the first time in my life my mother's admonition that I chew thirty times after every bite. Now and again I took a very small sip of Tang. Anything to delay the actual moment of getting in the rafts, thereby postponing *drowning* in the rapids.

A small rock whizzed through the air, skipping three times in water before disappearing into the dun-colored river. Jess stood beside me, shading his eyes with one hand.

"I wondered where you were," he said. "What happened, did Mike drive you away with all that harmonica playing?"

"Oh, no, I enjoyed it." I nearly choked on a mouthful of pancake.

Jess laughed, watching my expression. "Rates right up there with nails scraping on a chalkboard, doesn't it? I think he imagines himself as kind of a musical cowboy, giving us all a touch of atmosphere around the old camp fire. It never occurs to him that he might be giving us indigestion to go along with it."

"I've certainly never met anyone like him," I said cautiously. It was evident that Jess adored his uncle despite his idiosyncrasies. Had it been my uncle who was dressing up in Mickey Mouse hats and serenading my friends with a harmonica, I would have taken the first bus out of town. At night.

"He's one in a million," Jess said quietly. "I know he

can be sort of overbearing at times, but his bark is a lot worse than his bite." He paused, golden-brown eyes glinting. "He and I have something in common, you know."

"Don't tell me." My neck was getting a kink from looking up at him. I stood carefully, balancing my plate in one hand and my Dixie cup in the other. "You play the harmonica too."

His smile widened, sending my pulse thumping. He stepped closer, his sandals nudging my Adidas sneakers in the sand. "We're habit-forming," he said. "The more you know us, the more you love us."

He stared at me intently, his eyes seeming to touch every mosquito bite on my face. My nose began to itch.

"Chelsea?" He touched my hair, tucking a strand carefully behind my ear.

"What?" Nervously I raised my drink to my mouth. His hand captured my wrist in midair.

"There's a fly swimming in your Tang," he said gently.

Openmouthed with astonishment, I looked. There was indeed a fly swimming in my Tang. It was the size of Milwaukee, with black pipe-cleaner legs and quivering waterlogged wings.

"I'm going to be sick," I said softly. "I could have swallowed it. I could have *chewed* it."

Grinning, Jess took the cup from my hand and tossed its contents over a straggly weed. "You would never have known. You'd probably have thought it was orange pulp or something."

"Tang doesn't have pulp!"

"It does when you're camping," he replied cheerfully. "Mike wanted to get an early start this morning. Have you finished your breakfast?"

I looked down at my half-eaten pancake. If Tang had flies, who knew what could be hidden in a pancake? "Yes, I'm done. I don't think I could eat another bite."

He gestured grandly toward the camp with my empty

Dixie cup, uncoiling a smile that turned my kneecaps to water. Pearly Ultra-Brites in a Coppertone face. "After you, princess. Your barge awaits."

I walked slowly, trying not to stumble over the lumpy ground. No matter how carefully I held my plate, I kept sloshing maple syrup over the rim and onto the toes of my sneakers. Tossing the plate in the river or throwing it into the bushes was simply out of the question. Mike Calahan had instructed us that all paper plates and cups were to be disposed of in the fire. Anyone caught littering would face the punishment of being "split, skinned, and hung by the ears." I wasn't at all sure he was jesting, and I had no desire to find out.

Mike was standing over the dying fire when we returned, his harmonica suspended by a leather cord around his neck. The duffel bags had been loaded onto the rafts, and all other signs of our stay in the small clearing had been removed. Near the water's edge Sandy and Ranger were strapping life jackets on wiggling Boy Scouts.

Mike looked up and glared beneath his bushy brows. "Nice of you to join us," he boomed, the harmonica jumping on his massive chest. "We thought we might like to spend a little time on the river today. Is that all right with you?"

I squirmed uncomfortably under his piercing gaze. "I didn't realize it was so late," I apologized weakly. "I sort of lost track of the time."

Mike ignored my apology, zeroing in on my half-eaten breakfast. "Looks like you lost your appetite too. Never had any complaints about my buckwheat pancakes before, Hyatt. Don't tell me you're one of those girls who lives on lettuce leaves and bean sprouts? I'll never understand anyone who is willing to ruin their health just to get rid of a few extra pounds."

I threw my plate into the fire. "I am not on a diet," I said. "I wear a size five *petite.*"

"It's eating all that rabbit food," Mike replied, shaking his head in disgust. "Back when I was young, we appreciated a solid woman. None of those anemic-looking misses you see nowadays. Finicky eaters, the lot of them."

Now I was anemic. Jess had been totally wrong about Mike Calahan. The longer I knew him, the less I liked him.

"There was a fly swimming in my drink," I said stiffly. "I enjoy a good source of protein as much as the next person, Mr. Calahan, but I draw the line at swallowing flies. It sort of ruined my appetite."

Mike exchanged a look with Jess, who was grinning from ear to ear. "A fly in her drink?" he asked, eyes opening very wide beneath the yellow headband.

Jess nodded. "Uh-huh."

I closed my eyes and waited, knowing what Captain Bligh would say next.

"What was he doing?" Mike asked. "Backstroke or butterfly?"

Once in the raft, I wedged myself between Cameron and a duffel bag and tried to ignore the sounds of my stomach growling. I had no idea how long it would be before we reached the rapids, but I was determined to be prepared. Yesterday's dunking had taught me never to lower my guard against a sneaky river.

Jess used the paddles to guide us away from shore and into the current, then relaxed in the front of the raft and traded fish stories with a couple of the scouts. The morning sunlight reflected off the sandstone cliffs, highlighting the satin-red bodies of the insects that skittered over the water's surface. Directly ahead of us, poor Sandy and Ranger traveled with Captain Bligh and his harmonica. I couldn't hear very well over the murmuring of the river, but it sounded like he was entertaining them with a variety of polka pieces.

I quickly lost interest in the conversation around me,

which consisted of phrases such as "wallhangers on a salmonfly lure" and "snagging a lunker on your line." I listened instead for the ominous rumblings that would warn me of the appraching rapids. Even to my ultrasensitive ears the river seemed unusually calm and peaceful.

Jess laughed at something one of the scouts had said, drawing my eyes to the front of the boat. Staring at Jess had been the one thing I'd tried to avoid since I'd realized it was the one thing I really wanted to do. Translation: If you like someone, don't be caught staring at him or he might guess your guilty secret. But I had already counted the duffel bags in the boat, read the guarantee on the life preserver I wore—it claimed to be made of the highest quality materials but made no promises about saving my life—and smeared suntan oil over my arms and legs. I had run out of distractions.

His head was thrown back, the sunlight tangling in his hair and gilding the strong, brown column of his throat. He lounged carelessly against the pontoon, broad shoulders silhouetted against the gray-blue water. Then his laughter ended in a deep chuckle, and he turned his head, catching and holding my eyes with his own.

I was taken by surprise. It was my only excuse for sitting there like a statue while his gaze turned my bones to soggy toast. And before I looked away, the blood boiling in my cheeks, I had slipped painlessly into Stage One.

There was no need to panic. Falling in and out of love with great regularity as I did, I was well acquainted with Stage One. Years ago, when Sandy and I had first begun taking an interest in the opposite sex, we had catalogued the mysterious process of falling in love. Stage One: infatuation, my specialty. Stage Two: friendship and mutual admiration. Stage Three: physical attraction. And last but not least, Stage Four. This, of course, was undying and eternal devotion. Sandy claimed to be firmly stuck in Stage Four, with my brother as the unlikely object of her affections. I had never been beyond Stage One myself, but Sandy told me I would recognize it when it happened.

As I said, there was no need to panic. I busied myself studying the fascinating puddles of muddy water on the floor of the raft, my pulse keeping time with Mike's lively harmonica playing. Out of the corner of my eye I saw Jess rise and make his way toward me, expertly dodging an attempt by one of the scouts to push him out of the boat.

Long ago Cameron had vacated his seat beside me to take up the position of lookout on top of the supplies. Jess took his place, casually stretching his arm along the pontoon behind my back. He wore no shirt beneath his life jacket, and when his bare shoulder brushed mine, I felt a jolt of electricity shoot clear to my toes.

"Did I mention that I'm also the social director for this cruise?" he asked, leaning his head against the pontoon and closing his eyes.

"I don't think so." My stomach gurgled in the silence.

"Well, I am. Which means that it is my responsibility to make sure that everyone on board has a good time." One eye opened lazily, squinting up at me. "You, princess, are not having a good time."

An hour ago I would have told him that he was absolutely right. I hadn't slept in thirty hours, I was starving to death, and I had been contaminated with fly germs.

But that was before Stage One. Falling in love can do wonderful things for your endurance.

"Of course I am," I lied bravely. "What makes you think I'm not?"

"Oh, little things," Jess replied thoughtfully. "You've been curled up alone in the back of this boat all morning. You haven't said a single word to anyone, and your face is the color of cream cheese. Even Cameron noticed." Jess smiled, his eyes moving toward the lone figure in blue atop the supplies. "He told me he thought you were seasick. He decided he would be safer on high ground."

"I'm not sick," I reassured him. "If I'm pale, it's just because I'm a little . . . nervous. When I get nervous, all the blood goes to my head or something." I was babbling and I knew it, but I couldn't seem to stop. "Ranger took me to see *Poltergeist* last summer. I passed out in my seat halfway through the show. When I came to, the movie had just ended and the lights were coming on. I'd been out cold, and Ranger hadn't even noticed."

"Knowing Ranger, that doesn't surprise me," Jess said dryly. "So what is it that's making you so nervous?"

Unfortunately there was no need to answer. The river did it for me. Suddenly the peaceful, whooshing sound I had heard all morning changed to something more intense, a sort of rumbling that seemed to ricochet off the cliffs. Within seconds the rumbling grew to a roar, and the boat slipped faster through the water. The flashing, long-legged insects that had played so lazily on the surface disappeared in a line of mist that rolled over us like a fogbank. Scouts began to jump and shriek with excitement and the boat pitched wildly.

I forgot how to breathe. My hand clamped like a vise on the puffy material of Jess's life jacket.

"Chelsea, listen." Jess pried my fingers from his jacket, threading them through his own. There was a smile in his voice. "I swear to you, there is nothing to be scared of. If there was any sort of danger, do you think we'd even be on this river? Just do what I say, and everything will be fine. Who knows, you might even enjoy yourself. Most people think running the rapids is the best part of the whole trip."

Even in my panic I registered the fact that most guys wouldn't have been so patient. Ranger, for instance, would have thrown cold water in my face and told me to snap out of it. I appreciated Jess taking the time to try to reassure me, even though I didn't believe a word he said. I also enjoyed the feeling of his hand clasped in mine. It was a shame I was going to drown before I had a chance to really get to know him.

"Come on." Jess pulled me to my feet. Once out of the pontoon's protection, the mist in my face turned to spray and I was drenched in seconds. Jess grinned down at me, his hair splayed in a dripping, dark blond mat over his forehead. "Are you going to pass out on me?"

"No." Didn't they say that positive thinking was half the battle?

"Come on up front. I want you where I can see you. Cameron, stow your binoculars in your duffel bag. Zack, Chris, you two get in the back and secure the tarp over the supplies. Ryan, pull the paddle in or we'll lose it."

The next few minutes passed in a blur. I followed instructions like a robot, checking knots on the supply ropes (they looked fine to me) and securing anything that happened to be loose in the raft. I glowed like a beacon when Jess bestowed an absentminded "Good girl" on me. It became increasingly tricky to keep my balance on the lurching floor of the raft. Eventually I sank to my knees on the cold rubber, fear-frozen hands clutching the slippery pontoon. Most of the scouts were following my example, their exhilaration fading to wide-eyed apprehension.

Jess had climbed onto the edge of the boat, as if he were riding a horse, one foot tucked under the rim of the pontoon, the other under the boat in the water. Water rushed over his legs as the boat and the river moved faster. He had a paddle in his hand and a look of pure joy on his face. I gaped at him dumbly, wondering how on earth he got the courage to sit on the rim of the boat as the Colorado boiled around his knees.

There was a thundering in my ears as the river changed from water with a sense of direction to egg whites in a ten-speed blender. The boat pitched suddenly toward the sky and then swooped down on the churning foam. I slammed my nose against the pontoon. A spray of water hit me full in the face, taking my breath away and blurring my vision. I could hear Jess shouting at me, but before I had time to respond, the boat heaved again and left me facedown in three inches of muddy water.

I grabbed the supply rope and pulled myself to my knees, muttering some four-letter words I had been spanked for using ten years earlier. Now I was getting mad. It was one thing to meet an untimely end by being capsized or washed out of a boat. But I refused to drown in a lousy *puddle*.

The boat leveled long enough for me to turn my head and count scouts. They were all there, on hands and knees and stomachs and backs, the sound of their laughter lost in the roaring river. Cameron, to my amazement, was straddling the rim of the boat just as Jess did, a wide smile pushing at his sunburned cheeks.

"Hold on to the rope," Jess yelled at me. "Brace your feet against the pontoon."

I did as I was told, catching my breath as the boat glanced off a boulder and spun in a narrow, dizzying circle. Jess dug a paddle into the water and held it there until we were facing downstream again. Then the boat rushed forward with a lurch that sent my stomach into my throat. Gradually I became adjusted to the white water's rhythm. We climbed toward the sky in slow motion, floated in midair, and dropped like a stone. Then it started again. Jess hadn't been far from the truth when he described this as the wildest roller-coaster ride in the world. It certainly seemed like the longest.

When the churning water had finally subsided to lively, foam-flecked eddies, Jess motioned for me to grab a paddle and climb onto the rim of the pontoon. "It'll be a good experience for you," he said. "If something ever happened, you should know how to turn the boat and get it to shore." He grinned, his vivid eyes twinkling, and added, "Close your mouth, princess. You'll get flies in your teeth. If Cameron can do it, so can Chelsea."

He had a point, much as I hated to admit it. I should know something about the boat beyond how to hold on to it. I glanced back at Cameron, who sat proudly on the pontoon, his bony little shoulders square beneath his dripping shirt.

Even cream puffs had their pride.

I rose clumsily, my legs wriggling like Jell-O. I pulled a paddle from beneath the rim of the pontoon and carefully —oh, so carefully—slid my leg over the edge.

"Grip with your knees," Jess instructed. "Choke up on the paddle so it doesn't slip out of your hands. Good. You're a natural."

I would have doubled over laughing if I wasn't so afraid of losing my balance. The Colorado looked far friendlier now, but I still wasn't keen to repeat yesterday's humiliation.

Having experienced firsthand the violent moods of the river, I listened intently to every word Jess said. By the time we caught up to Mike and the others and pulled over to shore for lunch, Jess had pronounced me second-in-command, assistant scoutmaster, and most-improved river rat.

I had no idea whether I could actually keep my head in an emergency. I only knew I didn't want the chance to find out.

We ate ham-and-cheese sandwiches for lunch—filet mignon to my empty stomach. Sandy and I sat on our life jackets on the rocky shore, separated from the others by an enormous uprooted cottonwood tree that had somehow been thrown onto the riverbank. Its trunk was four feet in diameter, the huge root system at least twice that. I tried to imagine the amount of force necessary to uproot such a tree and shivered. Perhaps I hadn't yet seen the worst the Colorado had to offer.

"Oh, I wish you could have seen Ranger." Sandy giggled, licking the traces of a Ding-Dong from her fingers. "He sailed through the rapids like a pro, yelling instructions at everyone, helping Mike turn the boat, reassuring me that everything was under control. And then, *then*, when we were three feet from shore, he tripped over a paddle and fell backward into the water. I've never laughed so hard in all my life."

"Serves him right," I told her. "The little weasel hasn't let me forget for a minute my dunking yesterday. I only wish you could have taken a picture. I'd frame it and hang it on the living room wall." I took off my shoes, brushing the sticky grit from the soles of my feet. "Oh, cripes! Will you look at this? I've got drowned bugs between my toes."

"He kissed me last night," Sandy said suddenly.

For the second time that day my jaw dropped. I remembered Jess's comment about catching flies and shut it quickly. "Who kissed who?"

"Ranger, stupid. Who else?"

"*Ranger*?"

"Don't look so suprised," Sandy replied indignantly. "I'm not completely unattractive, you know."

"It's not that, " I hastened to reassure her. "It's just that . . . good grief, I didn't think he knew how."

Sandy sighed, looking out over the water with a blissful smile. "Oh, he does. Believe me, he knows how."

I absorbed this for a moment. My brother a Romeo? Could this be the same person who practiced bird calls on our roof and kept a poster of Woodsey the owl in his bedroom? Amazing. No, it was beyond amazing. It was truly incredible.

"Who would have guessed?" I murmured finally. "You and Ranger Rick, after all this time."

"Thanks to you," Sandy put in happily. "I would never

have signed up for this river trip if you hadn't agreed to come along. I owe you one, Chelsea.''

"No. You don't owe me anything.'' Automatically my eyes strayed to a certain golden-blond head. "It hasn't been so bad, all things considered. Sandy?''

"Mmmmfph?'' Her mouth was full of Shasta.

"What would you say if I told you . . .'' My voice trailed off uncertainly. What was there to tell, after all? That I had another one of my famous crushes on the only eligible male for miles? I didn't want Sandy comparing Jess with the long line of boyfriends I had discarded along the way. Admittedly I wasn't exactly known for remaining true-blue to one boy for any length of time. It seemed I was always attracted to those macho athletic types who looked adorable in football jerseys. I was a sucker for a shirt with a number on it. Unfortunately it only took two or three dates before I discovered the sad truth. Either he had a room-temperature IQ or he made more passes in the backseat than he did on the football field. Incomplete passes, I might add.

But Jess was different. Not only was he good-looking, but also he had a sense of humor and a *niceness* that even outshone his looks.

Of course, there was no reason in the world why Jess should be interested in *me*. I hadn't exactly impressed him with my outdoor skills in the past two days. And unless he had a fetish for girls with bugs between their toes and hair like a Brillo pad, it wouldn't be my looks that won him over.

"Told me what?'' Sandy repeated curiously.

"Nothing.'' I smiled brightly and raised my can of Shasta to the sky. "Here's to Mike Calahan's harmonica. May it be washed overboard and rust forever at the bottom of the Colorado.''

"Amen,'' Sandy said fervently. "Amen.''

Chapter 5

The river reverted to an innocent babbling brook for the rest of the afternoon. I curled up with my head on a duffel bag and watched lazily as Cameron coaxed Jess into a game of poker. The night I had spent tossing and turning was catching up with me. The sun felt warm on my eyelids, and the gentle rocking motion of the raft lulled me into a deep, dreamless sleep.

When I opened my eyes again, a cool breeze was raising goose bumps on my arms, and the sky was red with a watercolor sunset. I realized that the jerky movements of the raft dragging on sand had awakened me.

"It's about time," Cameron said from somewhere above me. "You missed all the excitement."

I blinked him into focus, then turned my head and peered sleepily over the pontoon. Jess had jumped out to anchor us on shore. I watched the muscles rippling in his arms and asked dreamily, "What excitement?"

"I beat Jess at poker. Twelve times." Cameron was nearly jumping up and down with joy. "I won seven dollars, a bag of licorice, and a compass. You wanna play tonight?"

"You think I'm crazy?" I said, getting stiffly to my feet. I could feel the river swaying beneath me, even though the raft was resting on solid ground. Some distance up the shore I saw Mike's empty boat, beached on a heap of glinting silver rocks. "Where is everybody?"

"They went to check out Chicken Cliff. That's where we're going." Cameron ducked as three blue blurs leapt over us onto the shore. I practiced putting names to faces as they raced into the trees: Zack, a blond kid with a Prince Valiant haircut; Chris, the quiet one with the sweet smile; and What's-his-name with the runny nose. Ryan. Boy Scouts in uniform were kind of like potatoes. They were all different, but it was tough distinguishing one from the other.

"Sounds exciting," I said, stifling a yawn.

"Jess says it doesn't look like much from here, but it's awesome from above. Wanna come?"

"Later. You go ahead." I waved Cameron on and struggled out of my life jacket. I couldn't understand all the fuss being made about some cliff, particularly if it was uninspiring enough to be named after poultry. Of course, I could be misjudging it. Maybe it was some type of stone formation that looked like a chicken or had petroglyphs from the ancient Indians. In that case, I'd wait for the morning light to see it and take my Kodak Instamatic along. In the meantime I was finally alone with Jess. When you're traveling with a group of Boy Scouts, opportunities like this are few and far between.

I still had my sea legs, and I was wobbling as I walked up the beach. Jess folded his arms across his chest and watched my progress, grinning as I stumbled over thin air.

"I wondered when you were going to wake up," he said. "Welcome back, princess."

"It's nice to be here," I said politely. I leaned heavily against the tree trunk he had used to anchor the raft. "It will be even nicer when the ground stops rocking beneath my feet."

"It gets easier." Jess laughed. "Give yourself a few minutes and you'll be back on land again."

"They didn't seem to have this problem," I pointed out, nodding toward the trees behind which Cameron and his buddies had disappeared.

"They were too excited to notice. Chicken Cliff is the high point of the trip for these guys. They couldn't wait to get a look at it. How about you? Don't you want to see what you'll be up against in the morning?"

I stared at him, feeling the first faint stirrings of alarm. Could this Chicken Cliff possibly be named for its inhabitants? Some sort of wild chicken we were expected to—to what?

"I think I might have missed something here," I said slowly. "Just what *is* Chicken Cliff?"

"If you hadn't slept all afternoon," Jess said, "you would know. It's all we talked about while you were snoring."

"I do not snore!"

"All right. Maybe snoring is too strong a word." Jess paused, considering. "You wheeze."

I was not willing to debate the issue, particularly when I had a sneaking suspicion that he was right. Ranger often told me that when I was extremely tired, my snores could be heard from the other end of the house. "Chicken Cliff," I reminded him darkly.

"Oh, yes." Jess took my hand in his, pulling me away from my nice steady tree trunk. "Come on. I'll show you."

We followed the shoreline past Mike's boat and around a thick outcrop of aspen trees. I would have been perfectly content if we had walked along the Colorado forever. Fading sunlight fell through the arch of trees, warming my back through my thin cotton shirt. The river lapped timidly at the shore, apologizing for all the terror and humiliation it had put me through during the past two days. Jess's fingers were threaded through mine, and the simple act of holding hands rendered me speechless. I loved the scraggly-looking flowers that grew in clumps beneath the aspen trees, loved the birds in the trees and the fish in the river. I took a deep breath of the fresh mountain air and tumbled headfirst into Stage Two.

Sandy had been right. It wasn't hard to recognize this stage at all. It was simply feeling comfortable with someone, knowing you didn't need words to fill the silence. I didn't have to babble or flutter my eyelashes or worry about the sorry condition of my hair. My feet were floating six inches above the ground, a side effect I reminded myself to tell Sandy about later. Apparently weightlessness comes along with friendship and mutual admiration.

"There it is," Jess said as we rounded a bend. "Chicken Cliff, in all her glory."

It didn't look glorious to me. It looked like a sheer piece of rock topped with a bunch of furry green trees. It wasn't even an impressive cliff, being only twenty-five or thirty feet high. It rose straight out of the river and put an abrupt end to the beach. I had seen office towers that were more inspiring.

"It's just a cliff," I said lamely.

Jess sighed. "You have no imagination. Look again."

I looked. No petroglyphs, no rock formations. If there were any wild chickens around, they were in hiding. "I'm sorry. I just don't see what all the excitement is about. It's no different from all the other cliffs we've seen in the last two days."

"That's where you're wrong." Jess put his arm around my shoulder, and when he spoke, his breath tickled my ear. "Look at the water directly under the cliff. See how it's darker than the rest of the river?"

I nodded, not trusting myself to speak. My heart had kicked into double time, and I had completely forgotten how to exhale. I once read that if you blow into a horse's ear, he'll follow you anywhere. Now I believed it.

"That's because it's deep," Jess went on. "Very deep. And there's a current running through there that's much warmer than the rest of the river. All in all, it's just perfect for cliff diving."

I thought I'd heard him wrong. I *must* have heard him wrong. I looked at him sideways and forced a hollow laugh. "I thought you said cliff diving."

"I did. Every time we take a trip down the river we make a point of stopping here. We take a whole morning just to swim and laze around. We use Chicken Cliff as a high dive."

All thoughts of romance and horses and ticklish ears went up in smoke. My smile froze on my face, and the hairs on the back of my neck stood up. I forced my eyes slowly upward, gazing at the cliff that had suddenly taken on the proportions of Mount Everest. Had Ranger been there, he would have recognized my sudden paralysis for what it was—pure terror. I had always had an intense, uncontrollable fear of high places. Our doctor called it acrophobia. Ranger called it stupid. I got dizzy sitting on the top bleachers in the school gymnasium. I shook like a leaf walking down open stairwells. I even broke out in a cold sweat riding in elevators, just thinking about the empty shaft below me.

In other words, I was a basket case. A chicken, after which this blasted cliff was named.

"This is where we baptize our river rats," Jess was saying. "It's a tradition with Calahan Expeditions. Everyone we bring down the Colorado takes a plunge off Chicken Cliff."

"What about those senior citizens you told me about?" I asked weakly, grasping at straws. "Surely they didn't have to—"

"Oh, they didn't *have* to." Jess grinned. "They wanted to. Every single one of them sailed off that cliff like they were stepping into a warm bath. They were great sports."

Doom. A seventy-five-year-old great-grandmother could take a leap, but Chelsea Anne Hyatt couldn't. I was developing a nasty habit of getting myself into humiliating situations. What would Jess Calahan think of me when I went bonkers on top of Chicken Cliff?

A flash of orange on the top of the cliff caught my eye. Ranger appeared, motioning to someone behind him. A minute later the ledge was swarming with scouts.

Cameron saw us and waved his hands wildly. "Come on up!"

"How about it?" Jess turned his head, squeezing my shoulder lightly. "Would you like to see the view from the top? There's a trail that winds up the back of the cliff. If we hurry, we can make it up and back before we lose the light."

"Oh, I think I'll wait till tomorrow," I said vaguely. "You go ahead. I'll go . . . start the fire or something."

Jess looked startled. "On the off-chance that you set the mountain on fire," he said finally, "I think I'll stay by the water."

We walked back along the beach, gathering armloads of driftwood as we went. After pointing out a good place to build the fire, Jess stretched out on the ground, leaning his back against a tree trunk. His expression clearly said, *It's all yours, princess.*

I gathered the largest stones I could find, dragging, rolling, and shoving them into a circle. I broke three nails and stubbed my toe, but it was a terrific way to release a little nervous energy. So far, so good.

I piled the wood we had gathered in a heaping mound

within the circle. Then I remembered I hadn't used any small twigs at the bottom for tinder. I removed the wood, threw in all the twigs and dried leaves I could find, and covered them up with the wood. My first fire, not counting the doughnuts I had set ablaze in Mom's deep-fat fryer.

I looked at Jess. He was smiling like the Cheshire cat, chewing on a blade of grass. He reached inside his pocket and tossed me a book of matches.

The wind had risen, blowing up from the river in sporadic gusts. I hunched over the wood, lighting one match after another. As soon as the flame flickered to life the wind put it out again. I changed positions, keeping my back to the river, and used up a dozen more matches before Jess knelt down beside me.

"It takes a little practice," he said. He struck a match against a rock and, cupping it with his hands, set fire to the tinder. We both stepped back as the fire blazed into life, casting its flickering shadow along the length of the rocky beach.

"I did pretty well for a beginner." I smiled at Jess proudly. I was fairly certain I had dirt smudged on my face and leaves caught in my hair, and I didn't even care. "Hey, how'd you like to keep me around permanently? I could be the official fire builder for Calahan Expeditions."

As soon as the words were out of my mouth I could hardly believe I'd said them. Keep me around permanently . . . it sounded like I was asking him to marry me or something. What if Jess didn't realize I was only kidding?

But Jess didn't seem concerned. He smiled and said quietly, "I think I'd like that."

His gaze drifted down to my mouth, and the atmosphere between us changed subtly and unmistakably. Suddenly I noticed the laugh lines that framed his mouth, the way his hair curled over his ears, the pulse that beat steadily at the base of his throat. I wondered if he was seeing me with the same astounding clarity. I hoped not.

His hand slipped beneath my hair and cupped my neck, drawing me slowly toward him. "You've got a smudge on your nose," he said, a soft inflection in his voice.

"Yes." The word barely escaped my desert-dry mouth. The matchbook slid from my fingers and landed on the ground. Jess was going to kiss me. It was my next-to-last thought as his head bent to mine. My last thought was a fervent prayer that my knees wouldn't buckle.

"Hey, you guys! Look what I found!"

It was Cameron, crashing through the foliage like a demented buffalo. Jesse and I sprang apart, putting a good five feet between us before we stopped scrambling. I looked at the fire, the sky, my shoelaces. Anywhere but at Jess. I wanted to cry. Did fate have it in for me? My knees didn't even get a chance to buckle.

"It's an eagle feather," Cameron informed us proudly. His attention was focused solely on the scrawny white feather he carried. He moved closer to the fire, offering his treasure to Jess for inspection. "I found it on top of Chicken Cliff. Did you know it's good luck to find an eagle feather?"

"No." Jess sighed. "Are you sure about that?"

"Sure I'm sure. Mike told me. Hey, Chelsea! You should have climbed up there with us. You can see clear down the canyon. It's like being in an airplane or something. I swear. You're coming up tomorrow, aren't you?"

The kid was a menace. While I was staring at him, wondering how to get out of this, Mike and the others returned. I took advantage of the opportunity and quickly offered to help unload the boats, much to Ranger's amazement. There was a method to my madness. I didn't want Cameron—or anyone else, for that matter—asking me about Chicken Cliff. I hadn't formulated my strategy yet, but I was determined to keep my feet on solid ground tomorrow without looking like a coward.

We ate steaming bowls of beef stew around the camp

fire and roasted marshmallows on green willow sticks. I didn't notice the cold or even the mosquitoes that zeroed in for their dinner from miles around. I watched Jess from beneath my lashes and felt a warm glow whenever he smiled at me. I kept remembering the brief shadow of his mouth over mine and that exquisite moment of anticipation before Cameron and his eagle feather happened on the scene. I never, ever wanted to come back to earth again.

That night I dreamed that my mother sent me out to hunt chickens. She wanted to make chicken croquettes. She gave me a bow and the kind of arrow that was made out of plastic with a little rubber suction cup on the end. Then she pushed me out our front door, which just happened to open onto the edge of Chicken Cliff.

I looked down and saw the rapids, their churning white foam crashing over boulders and uprooting gigantic trees. The horribly familiar terror washed over me in waves, closing off my breathing. The ground heaved beneath my feet. And then I was falling, tumbling head over heels into the raging river below. . . .

I opened my eyes with a gasp, heaving a shuddering breath when I realized I was not about to meet my doom in the Colorado. *It was a dream, Chelsea. Only a dream.*

But the fear had been very real. My trembling fingers plucked pyramids into my sleeping bag as I stared up at the pale gray sky. The stars were dull and fading, blinking out one by one. I knew from experience that if I went back to sleep, the dream would return.

It was still an hour or two until dawn. I pulled a flashlight and a paperback from my duffel bag and began chapter one of *Rapture's Revenge.*

It looked like it was going to be easier than I'd thought. After breakfast everyone changed into their swimsuits, then made a mad dash for Chicken Cliff. Sandy and I changed into our suits, too, using our sleeping bags as dressing rooms. She wore a lemon-yellow bikini that showed off her tan, and I wore a silvery, figure-hugging maillot that made Jess's mouth drop open when he saw it.

"Catching flies?" I asked innocently. I was rewarded with a smile that brought a sudden warmth to my face.

I was very self-confident this morning. I had a *plan*. The scouts were already leaping off Chicken Cliff. Their shrieks and giggles and war cries could be heard from one end of the gorge to the other. I told Sandy, Ranger, and Jess to go on without me, that I would join them as soon as I had finished helping Mike clean up the dishes from breakfast. I could tell by the look on Ranger's face that he was getting suspicious. It simply wasn't in my nature to volunteer. But Sandy had been briefed earlier and knew exactly what to do. She took Ranger by one hand and Jess by the other and hustled them quickly out of the camp.

If my mother ever found out the method used to clean dishes on a river trip, she would have a coronary. We scooped up dry sand and rubbed it around on the soiled dish for about thirty seconds. Then we dumped off the sand, wiped the plate clean with a paper towel, and packed it away. *Voilà*. Not very sanitary, but it did conserve water.

After the dishes were done Mike stretched out in a hammock he had tied between two pine trees. He mumbled something about "forty winks" and pulled his Mickey Mouse cap down over his face. I was elated. As far as my plan was concerned, Mike Calahan couldn't have been more cooperative if he'd tried.

There was no one to see me when I grabbed my life jacket and set out on the same path Jess and I had taken the night before. I ran quickly along the beach, being very careful to stick close to the trees. It was more painful on my bare feet than the sand near the riverbank would have been, but at least I was hidden from whoever happened to be jumping off Chicken Cliff.

It worked like a charm. No one even noticed when I slipped into the water. Scouts were dropping from Chicken Cliff like torpedoes, each wearing a life jacket that brought him bobbing back to the surface. There seemed to be no current at all in the small cove beneath the cliff. The scouts splashed and swam and dunked each other until they grew bored, then they scrambled out of the water and hiked back up the cliff again.

I couldn't see Jess, but I spotted Sandy and Ranger floating together in the shade of a shallow cavern that cut into the base of the cliff. Their foreheads were bent together, and they seemed oblivious to the bodies crashing into the water around them. I dunked my head and got my hair wet, then dunked a few scout heads until Sandy noticed me.

"Hey, Chelsea!" She followed the script, raising her voice so everyone could hear. "I didn't see you jump. What did you think of Chicken Cliff?"

"It was high." I laughed, enjoying the stunned expression on Ranger's face. "I don't think I'll try that again. Once is enough."

"You jumped?" he asked. "*You*?"

I didn't want to do any more lying than was absolutely necessary. "Do you think I'm a complete coward?" I asked, avoiding a direct answer. "For heaven's sake, even the scouts are jumping."

Just then Jess sailed out from the ledge above us, doing a double somersault before hitting the water. He came up sputtering, shaking the glistening drops of water from his hair and eyelashes. He saw me, grinned, and disappeared beneath the surface again.

Jaws. I turned and began thrashing my way to shore. I had traveled about two inches (I'd never been a very good swimmer) before I felt a hand close around my ankle and drag me under the water. I barely had time to hold my breath and plug my nose.

Jess was waiting for me when my life jacket brought me bouncing back to the surface. He was smiling like a triumphant little boy. "You swim like a cocker spaniel," he said. "Didn't anyone ever teach you to do anything but a doggie-paddle?"

"Of course they did." I blinked at him through my dripping bangs. "And, for your information, that wasn't a doggie-paddle. That was the Australian crawl."

"Never let an Australian hear you say that. You have a very . . . unique style. I only wish I could have seen you jump."

"You must have been climbing back up the cliff when I took the plunge." Another half truth. He *had* been climbing up the cliff, but my plunge had only been from a height of three inches. I began to feel a little guilty.

"It's kind of like flying, isn't it?" Jess covered the distance between us with two easy strokes. "Hey, have you seen the petroglyphs yet?"

"No, I haven't." I quickly latched on to a subject that had nothing to do with cliff diving. "I didn't know there were any around here."

"Come on. I'll show you."

We swam across the cove through the maze of bobbing scouts. Jess moderated his powerful crawl to keep time with my awkward sidestroke. We broke through the shadows beneath the cliff and waded out onto a rocky beach. I followed Jess's example and took off my life jacket, leaving it in the sun where it could dry.

"I'm f-freezing," I stuttered, nearly biting off my tongue with my clacking teeth. "Are these p-petroglyphs very f-far away?"

Jess took my hand, leading me around the giant-size boulders at the base of the cliff. "Not far. The sun will warm you up in no time."

Keeping the cliff to our left, we climbed steadily upward. Our progress was slow, as I was very careful to avoid stepping on anything that looked like it might stab, jab, or bite. After several minutes of tiptoeing through the pine needles, we came upon an enormous rock that looked something like the Pillsbury Dough Boy. It was squatty and smooth and had round indentations for eyes and a mouth. Two smaller stones on either side looked like pudgy little arms.

"I think this will do," Jess said thoughtfully. Then he put his hands around my waist and lifted me on top of the sun-warmed rock.

I twisted my head, looking for carvings in the cliff wall behind me. "Are we lost? I don't see any petroglyphs."

"There aren't any," Jess said. "I lied."

"Oh. You lied." Under the circumstances it was the best I could do.

"There aren't any Boy Scouts, either," he continued, spreading his palms flat on the rock on either side of my legs. "That makes up for the petroglyphs, don't you think?"

I was past thinking. It was all I could manage to draw air in and out of my sore lungs. My gaze was caught helplessly in his until his gold-tipped lashes closed. Then my eyes closed, and I felt his lips settle over mine, barely touching. It was a gentle kiss, a sweet "first-time" kiss. When he lifted his head, my lips were tingling.

"Chelsea." He had a way of saying my name that made it sound different. His hands were warm on my shoulders, and when he kissed me again, it wasn't gentle or sweet. Over the pulse buzzing in my ears I heard faint, unfamiliar warning bells. I could feel the smooth brown skin of his back beneath my fingertips and the hot sun on my bare arms. Dimly I registered the fact that I wanted to get closer. I *needed* to get closer, and it was this thought that finally made me pull away.

We stared at each other wordlessly, both of us breathing quickly and hard. I was grateful for the Pillsbury Dough Boy. If I hadn't been sitting down, I would have fallen down.

"I'm sorry," Jess whispered thickly. "I hope you don't—"

"I'm not sorry." My voice was faint. This was a first for me, being so honest and open about my feelings. With other boys I had always kept my cool, waiting until they committed themselves before I did. But Jess wasn't like other boys, and I wanted him to know how I felt.

Jess laughed, that wonderful husky sound that would always remind me of an unsullied mountain morning and a melting, summer-blue sky. He lifted me off the rock with heartwarming care and placed a swift kiss on my forehead. "Come on. I feel like flying."

We were halfway up the back of Chicken Cliff when it penetrated my slap-happy brain that Jess was taking me to the top. *The top.*

I dug my heels into the earth, pulling my hand out of his. "I really don't want to jump again," I said, hoping that he would attribute the tremors in my voice to the steep climb. "I'm sort of tired."

"Once more," Jess said. "We'll go off together, holding hands."

I was getting desperate. "I don't have my life jacket."

"I won't let anything happen to you," he promised. His smile could have roasted marshmallows. "Come on, princess. It'll be fun."

"No! I told you, I'm tired. I don't want to jump again, Jess."

He was silent for a moment. Then he grinned and put out his hand, tugging gently on a strand of my hair. "Okay, you win. You don't have to jump. Just walk up there with me. You can watch while I do my famous Calahan cannonball jump."

I hesitated, wringing my fingers. If I went to the top with him, surely I could stay back where I couldn't see over the ledge?

"Please," Jess coaxed. "I need moral support. The Calahan cannonball is a very difficult maneuver. Last time I lost my swimming trunks."

I tried to return his smile, but my cheeks were stiff. He took my hand again and we followed the winding, well-worn path until it leveled off into a pine-covered plateau. Through the curtain of trees I could hear little boys giggling and the occasional shout of "Geronimo!" as someone else took the plunge. I began to feel dizzy.

"You go ahead," I whispered. "I'll watch from here."

"You can't see anything that way. You have to at least get past the trees. Come on."

I stumbled over the tree roots rippling the ground, hanging back when I saw the bleached blue sky through the trees. Thin air. The cliff. I stopped dead in my tracks, and my hand closed fiercely around a sticky tree limb.

"I'm not going any farther," I said. I didn't recognize the sound of my own voice. It was cold and flat and hard.

"Oh, yes, you are." Before I knew what was happening, Jess had lifted me into his arms and was carrying me through the dark green shadows. He was laughing, saying something about two of us jumping off the cliff together, whether Princess Chelsea liked it or not. Suddenly there were neither trees nor shadows, only the blazing white sunlight and a sheer, terrifying drop to the Colorado.

I tried to tell him, to blabber my fear like a baby, but no sound came out. I saw Cameron's freckled face silhouetted against the sky. He laughed at us, then held his nose and walked off the ledge.

"Ready?" Jess asked me. "One, two . . ."

My arm was made of lead. I lifted it in slow motion, digging my fingernails into the skin on Jess's shoulder. Tiny droplets of blood glittered in the sunlight.

"What the—" Jess looked at his shoulder, then at me. His face was flushed. "What the heck's the matter with you?"

He tried to put me down, to make me stand alone on the edge of that cliff. I finally found my voice. "No! Take me back! *Get back!*"

His face lost all expression. Very carefully he stepped backward, away from the edge. I closed my eyes tightly, holding on to him with all the strength I had. If I let go, I would fall. My dream would be real.

Jess didn't stop walking until he had put a screen of trees between me and the ledge. Then he set me gently on my feet and asked, "Why didn't you tell me?"

I was past rational thought. My senses were still reeling from shock, and I lashed out at Jess with all the fury that pure, unreasoning terror created. "Why did I think you were different? You're not! You don't understand anything! You're just like your uncle, crude and stupid and common! *I hate you!*"

And then I slapped him.

It wasn't the cool, crisp slap that you see in the movies. It landed sloppily on his chin, without enough force to even make him blink.

Jess just stood there with his hands balled into fists at his side. His face was pale, the skin stretched tightly over his cheekbones. In the silence that followed I started to cry.

Sandy and Ranger came up the path at that moment, freezing as they took in the scene.

"Help her," Jess said stiffly to Sandy. "She's been frightened."

"Jess . . . I'm sorry."

But he didn't hear my thin whisper. He was already gone.

Chapter 6

In between sobs and hiccups I told Sandy and Ranger everything that had happened. I omitted the part about kissing Jess, but I guess it was fairly obvious how much he meant to me. I tried to get up and go after him, but Ranger caught my arm and said it would be better if I gave Jess some time alone first. Then I could explain, and everything would be fine. Or so Ranger said.

We went back to camp and changed our clothes, then helped Mike load some of the gear into the boats. One by one the scouts came trudging back from Chicken Cliff, exhausted, dripping, and happy. I tried to smile at Cameron's story of a water snake that had scared him to death before he discovered it was a piece of driftwood. I lugged duffel bags and coolers from the camp to the rafts until my fingers were blistered and my back ached. I shrugged my shoulders when Mike asked me where Jess was and turned away before he could see the tears in my eyes.

I had never been so miserable in my life.

The boats were loaded and the supplies secured when Jess finally appeared. He offered no explanation for his absence and didn't even glance in my direction. When Mike told him we all had better things to do than sit around and twiddle our thumbs while we waited for "His Majesty," Jess gave him a grim look and said softly, "Why don't you just get off my back?"

It was the first time I had heard him talk to his uncle with anything but respect and affection. I knew it was all my fault, and I would have given anything to take back the ugly words I'd said.

I tried to approach Jess in the hectic moments when everyone was scrambling into the rafts. He was standing on the beach, coiling the rope that had anchored the boat during the night. His head was bent, and he didn't look up when I said his name.

"I want to apologize," I said.

"Forget it. There's no need to apologize." Still he didn't meet my eyes.

"Yes, there is!" I put my hand on his arm, only to take it away again when the muscles beneath my palm went rigid. "It was all my fault. I lied to you. I let you think that I had already jumped off Chicken Cliff. How were you to know the truth? Jess, look at me."

He did, but his eyes were cold and impersonal. "Chelsea," he said quietly, "I told you that I didn't need an apology. My mom has acrophobia. That's why she never spent any time with my dad in the mountains. If you had told me, I would have understood."

"I know. I know I should have told you." My voice was hoarse from crying. "It was just . . . I'd already done so many stupid things on this trip, and you were telling me how everybody jumped, even the senior citizens. I didn't want you to think I was a coward on top of everything else."

"I wouldn't have," he said. "You don't know me very well, do you, Chelsea?"

"I guess not." I blinked away stinging tears.

"Believe it or not, I'm capable of understanding quite a lot." He smiled at me, but it was a smile I didn't recognize. A stranger's smile.

"I didn't mean any of it," I said dully. "All those awful things I said—they didn't mean anything."

"Like I said, forget it." He finished coiling the rope and tossed it over his shoulder. "I asked Ranger to switch places with you in the raft today. I figured you'd be more comfortable with Sandy."

And that was the end of my humble apology, which was going to make everything all better. Like a kiss or a hug or a Band-Aid. Only this time I had hurt Jess too deeply to "make it all better." No matter how many apologies I made, those ugly things I'd said would still be there, hanging between us. For the first time in my life, being sorry wasn't enough.

It was close to noon before the rafts were finally out on the water again. Today they floated side by side, nearly motionless in the slow-moving current. For once the canyon walls weren't echoing with the sound of rambunctious boys. The scouts were sprawled over the duffel bags like dead fish, sleeping off the rigors of cliff diving. Even Mike was silent, sitting with both feet propped up on the pontoon and paddling only when the two boats drifted too close together.

Sandy and I sat together in the back of the raft, watching Chicken Cliff disappear in the distance. She was a good friend and allowed me to wallow in self-pity for quite a while before trying to cheer me up. As usual, when I'm depressed, I became a human garbage disposal. I ate Sandy's entire bag of cinnamon bears, all the leftover marshmallows, and the last of my own supply of M&M's. Then I began searching under the supply tarp for something else to stuff in my face. It was either that or start with the tears again.

"You're going to get fat," Sandy said finally. "And then Jess Calahan won't look at you twice."

I crawled back from under the tarp, carrying a miniature box of Sugar Smacks. "It doesn't matter. He'll never look at me again, anyway."

"That's where you're wrong. He's already looked at you ten to twelve times in the last five minutes."

Trying to be inconspicuous, I glanced at the other boat. Jess was stretched out in almost the same exact position as Mike. His eyes were closed. "He's asleep," I muttered, tossing a handful of Sugar Smacks into my mouth. "You must have been seeing things."

"He's pretending to be asleep," Sandy insisted. Then she grabbed the box of cereal from my hand, closed the lid, and sat on it. "You don't need any more food. You're going to be sick if you keep eating, and I don't want to be sitting next to you when it happens."

I didn't argue with her. I was already feeling a little queasy. "What time is it?"

Sandy consulted her watch. "Ten minutes later than the last time you asked. Why?"

I did some quick calculations. I have always been very good at math, something I generally keep quiet about. It's amazing how many boys are intimidated by a girl who takes advanced trigonometry. "We're scheduled to head for home at noon on Friday. That leaves forty-seven hours until this trip is officially over. I wonder if I'll last that long."

Sandy looked at me in disgust. "I don't believe you. Do you know what your problem is? You're spoiled!"

I shrugged my shoulders. I couldn't argue with that, either. My parents had always regretted the fact that they couldn't have more children. I knew they compensated for it by overindulging Ranger and me. "What's that got to do with anything? Are you still jealous because they let me redecorate my room?"

"No, you twit!" My dearest and best friend rolled her eyes to the sky. "I wasn't talking about that kind of spoiled. Besides, your room is pink and I don't even like pink."

"That wasn't what you told me," I said, wounded. "You said you loved the color. You even helped me pick out the wallpaper. Why didn't you tell me if you—"

"Will you shut up? Will you just shut up? I'm trying to make a point here, Chelsea Anne. When I said you were spoiled, I meant with boys. In the past all you had to do was click your fingers and they would come running like eager little puppies. And the pick of the litter was always yours for the asking."

I stared at her. "You've been working in the pet store too long."

"All right. Let me put it another way. It's like a pattern with you, Chelsea. No matter how many Prince Charmings you go out with, you always end up thinking they're frogs."

"Animals again."

"*You become bored with them,*" Sandy grated. "It never fails. Only this time it's different. This time—" she paused for effort—"this time you really care."

"So what's the point?" I asked miserably. "I mean, we both know I care about him, but that doesn't change anything. I blew it, Sandy. It's over. Kaput. Finished."

"Over?" Sandy fairly shrieked the word. One of the scouts lifted his head groggily and told us to put a lid on it. "Over?" she repeated, a decibel lower. "You fall in love with a guy and break it off again in three days? Doesn't that seem a little speedy, even for you? Chelsea, having a relationship with a guy isn't something that just happens. You have to work at it. That's your whole problem. You've never had to work at it before. If you care about Jess, really care about him, you ought to fight for him."

"You should write a column," I mumbled. "Sandy Landers."

"If you think about it," Sandy said gently, "you'll know that I'm right. Do you really want to go back to Denver and never see Jess again?"

I sniffed. "You know I don't."

"Then stop acting like a wet sponge. You've got"—she looked at her watch once again—"forty-six hours and fifty minutes to convince Jess Calahan that he can't live without you."

"But what if it doesn't work? I mean, maybe the guy just doesn't like me anymore. Have you thought of that?"

Sandy shrugged, propped her feet up on the pontoon, and closed her eyes. "There's always a risk when you care about somebody. I guess you just have to decide if he's worth it."

We hit white water again late that afternoon. I amazed myself. I actually got up on the rim of the boat like Jess had taught me and *paddled*. I had no idea whether my paddling was helping Mike or hindering him, but he never yelled at me, so I figured I must be doing it right. True, these rapids weren't quite as wild as yesterday's and they only lasted three or four minutes, but I was still proud of myself. I looked behind us to see if Jess had noticed, but his boat was invisible in the spray. I missed his pat on the back and his casual "Good girl." Boy, did I have it bad. Stage Five? Six? For all I knew I was breaking records.

"Will you look at that?" Mike said suddenly.

I glanced quickly at the river ahead, wondering with a sinking heart if we were in for more rapids. One exhibition of bravery a day was quite enough. "Look at what? I don't see anything."

"Not there. There." He pointed toward the shoreline,

which was thick with cottonwood and aspen trees. "Will you *look* at that?"

The trees rustled, and I saw two enormous brown eyes staring at us. A moment later the largest—and only—deer I had ever seen outside of a zoo stepped up to the water to drink. He was gigantic, almost the size of a horse, and his coat shimmered like mink. The raft fell silent and nearly capsized as everyone moved over to one side to look.

"I didn't know deer could get that big," I whispered. "Gosh, he's taller than I am."

"Not a deer," Mike said reverently. "No indeed. That fellow there is a bull elk. Full-grown. Just look at the size of those antlers."

The elk raised his head, as if to let me study his antlers. They were incredible, like two trees with a silky, mosslike coating. They seemed far too heavy for even that monster to carry around on top of his head. As I watched him he blinked, and even from that distance I could see the gentle brown eyes slowly close and open again. He seemed to be looking straight at me, and he was the most beautiful thing I had ever seen.

"We've driven the elk out with our cities and killed them off for sport," Mike said. "It's been close to ten years since I've seen one in these parts. I thought they were all gone."

"Why would anyone want to shoot something that special?" I asked softly. "How could they?"

Mike shrugged, pulling off his Mickey Mouse cap, and scratched his head. "I couldn't tell you. It's not the kind of hunting I can understand. Years back I couldn't walk five miles into these mountains without seeing the carcasses of two or three elk, shot for the fun of it and left to rot. 'Course, their heads would always be cut off. Men that kill for sport always like a trophy to display for their friends.

Nowadays it isn't quite so easy for them. They have to go farther and look longer before they can find their trophy. Still, I suppose they keep doing it."

I was surprised to find that I was close to tears again. It certainly seemed to be my day for crying. This time the tears had something to do with huge velvet-brown eyes and the thought that I would probably never see such an animal again. And in the back of my mind I began to understand Mike Calahan—and Jess—a little better.

"There should be laws," I said over the lump in my throat.

"There are laws, darlin'. Scads and scads of 'em, but never enough people to enforce them." He caught my misty-eyed look and, to my astonishment, took my hand in his. He smiled, the golden lights in his eyes reminding me of Jess. "You're looking like your pet poodle just tumbled under a garbage truck. Don't throw in the towel. We're a great people for waiting till the last minute and then pulling off a miracle."

It was the longest conversation I'd ever had with Mike Calahan. The only conversation, really. I thought I had him pegged as a bit of an oddball who liked to wear strange clothes and growl at people—when he wasn't annoying them with his harmonica playing. But suddenly I was seeing another side of him, a man who lacked the "social graces" but could talk about poodles and garbage trucks and miracles, all in the name of making Chelsea Anne Hyatt smile.

I wanted to thank him. My eyes lit on the harmonica dangling around his neck and I smiled.

"We haven't heard you play all day," I said. "Why don't you give us a song?"

We made camp that night on an island. Not a real island, of course, but a big chunk of sand and cottonwood trees set smack in the middle of the river. Mike called it a sandbar. He said it was the only place for miles where we could have pulled over for the night. During the afternoon the canyon walls on either side of the river had become so steep and sheer that they made Chicken Cliff look like a sand pile. They had also moved closer and closer to the water until finally there were no beaches at all. They rose straight from the river for as far as you could see, treeless sandstone monsters that had huge cavities in their bases where the river had eaten them away.

I asked Mike what would happen if our boat capsized and we had to get to shore—when there wasn't any shore. He just gave me one of his old bulldog looks and said it would be a real good idea *not* to capsize the boat for the next couple of days. " 'Cause, unless you're a human fly, darlin','' he added grimly, "there's no way out of the water but straight up.''

My eyes grew wide, and I began stuffing Oreos into my mouth. I also eat when I'm nervous.

Because of our delay in leaving Chicken Cliff that morning—I tried not to think about that—the sun was setting in red and violet streaks before we pulled over onto our island. Jess's boat was five or ten minutes behind us, and by the time they'd arrived, we had a fire made and most of our gear unloaded. Mike seemed to be in a great rush to get camp set up. I heard him tell Jess we were in for a storm before too long. I saw a few cotton-puff clouds floating around in the sky but nothing too ominous-looking. I decided Mike was probably being extra cautious since he was responsible for so many people.

Jess seemed to be in a better mood, laughing and joking with the scouts, but he never made any effort to speak to me. I caught him glancing in my direction once or twice, but when I smiled, he looked away. He wore a sleeveless white cotton jersey with a clown picture on the front. The words NO BOZOS ALLOWED were lettered beneath. Even in the dusky light I could see the narrow welts that my nails had made on his shoulder. I closed my eyes and turned away. When the temperature dropped and the wind came up, as it seemed to do every night in the mountains, he pulled on a navy blue windbreaker. I was grateful. Looking at his shoulder was a constant reminder of my stupidity.

Mike decided that we would put up our shelters before we ate. Up till now we had simply rolled out our bags on the most level piece of ground we could find and called it a night. But Mike was convinced that a storm was brewing, and he wanted everyone to have some protection. Had we been camped on the shore instead of the middle of the Colorado, we would have been able to find a cave or a rocky overhang to shelter us. Since that was impossible, we paired off and set up two-man tents.

Sandy and I looked at each other helplessly when Mike handed us a Barbie Doll-sized duffel bag and told us it was *ours*. Our very own tent, which we were apparently expected to put up.

All around us little scouts were erecting tents as if they were working on an assembly line. Ranger had disappeared into the trees to answer nature's call. Mike and Jess already had their tent up and were beginning preparations for dinner. It didn't seem to occur to anyone to give the ladies a hand. Chivalry was dead on the Colorado.

Sandy and I decided to accept the challenge. We had never had any experience putting up a tent before, but it certainly didn't appear to be complicated. Cameron, whom I assumed was sharing a tent with Ranger, had had his up and ready for occupancy in three minutes flat. Sandy timed him.

First we decided to be smarter than everyone else. We would move our tent closer to the trees where we'd have more protection. When the storm blew everyone else's tents into the river—providing there was a storm—we would still be snug and warm. How satisfying that would be.

We gave each other smug little grins and spread the contents of our duffel bag out on the ground as we'd seen Cameron do. We had a large piece of canvas, several lengths of thick twine, and a small pouch filled with metal and wooden stakes. If I could learn to French-braid my own hair (which was no simple feat), I could certainly put up a pup tent.

Using rocks for hammers, we pounded the metal stakes through the loops in the canvas and into the ground. We kept hitting cottonwood roots with the stakes and had to slant them every which way to get them all the way into the ground. They didn't look as professional as Cameron's, but they seemed secure enough. This took about thirty minutes. By now Jess had dinner cooking and we could smell the mouthwatering aroma of barbecued beef. We untangled our twine and threaded it through the metal rings in the canvas. Then we pulled it over to the stakes and back to the tent again. The finished product looked like a spiderweb, but at least we'd used up all of the twine. Finally we took the taller wooden stakes and propped them up inside the canvas. For a minute it seemed as if we had a real tent, and we were elated with our success. Then the wind came up, and the tent went down with a gentle little whoosh. After all our work, it was nothing but a puddle of canvas and twine at our feet. Sandy said a choice four-letter word, and I kicked dirt on the remains of our labor.

"That won't help," Jess said behind us. He was smiling faintly, staring at the disaster we had created. "Hasn't either one of you ever put up a pup tent?"

"I've heard of them," Sandy muttered, "but I always thought they were for dogs."

Jess choked back a laugh, but his eyes were brimming with humor. "Yeah, well . . . why don't I give you two a hand? Everyone else has already started eating. If we don't hurry, there won't be anything left. You know Ranger."

"Unfortunately," I said. Jess met my eyes with a grin, but there was nothing personal in his smile. It was the kind of smile he would give Cameron or Ranger, and it ended almost before it began.

"Listen up, ladies," he said.

Ten minutes later we were eating roasted corn-on-the-cob and barbecued ribs coated with a spicy, smoke-flavored sauce. I decided that watching Boy Scouts eat "finger food" had to be one of the most revolting sights on earth. They had barbecue sauce smeared from ear to ear and butter dripping from their little chins and noses. I asked Cameron if the Scout Oath included a promise never to use a napkin. He just grinned—a bit of corn was stuck between his two front teeth—and reached with a greasy hand for another rib.

Our tent now stood with all of the others, at some distance from the cottonwood trees. While he was helping us put it up, Jess had said exactly two sentences to me: "Hand me that stake" and "Tighten your slack." Without Sandy's pep talk earlier, I might have crawled into the bushes and indulged in another personal cloudburst. But she had made me realize something very important. I cared too much about Jess—all right, I *loved* him too much—to let things end like this. I didn't know if it was possible to make up for what I had said to him, but I had—roughly—forty-one hours and three minutes left to try.

After dinner Mike wanted to play us a selection of his favorite patriotic songs, but his harmonica had myster-iously disappeared. He compensated for that by reciting a poem about an old miner who lived in the hills with his pet raccoon. At the fifth or sixth verse Jess said he was tired and excused himself. I took a deep, fortifying breath, mumbled something about being pretty tired myself, and followed him.

Jess and Mike's tent was closest to the water, separated from the others by a small sandy knoll. When I caught up with Jess, he was standing at the river's edge, skipping stones over the water. His collar was pulled up against the chill, and the wind tossed restlessly through his hair. He looked . . . remote.

"Do you think I could do that?" I asked.

My voice startled him. He jumped about a mile high and dropped the rock in his hand. "Do what?"

"Skip stones. Will you show me?" I moved closer and picked up a stone from its sandy bed. "Is this one okay?"

"No." His voice was toneless. "It's got to be smooth and flat, like a pancake."

I searched until I found the right kind of rock. My heart was in my throat, and my fingers were trembling. I didn't really care if he noticed. "How's this one?"

"Fine. Now toss it"—he demonstrated quickly—"like that. Throw it the way you would a Frisbee, low on the water."

The moonlight shone full over the river and our little island. It glinted on Jess's hair and made the soft white of my sweater seem luminous. It also revealed the expression on Jess's face, which was none too encouraging. He looked polite, nothing more. I think I would have felt better if he'd still been angry with me.

I stepped to the water's edge and raised my arm to throw. Before I could let go of the rock, Jess grabbed me around the waist.

"You're too close," he said curtly. "We're not camped on the shore, Chelsea. This is a sandbar, and the current around us is fierce. If you fall in, you won't be able to doggie-paddle back to shore."

"Oh." I backed up and was disappointed when Jess let his hands drop from my waist. For one insane moment I thought he was going to hug me or rain kisses on my face or something. *Chelsea Anne, you've been reading too many romances.*

I threw my rock, and it sunk like the stone it was. I threw another one and another and another. They all sunk. Jess began to smile.

"It's impossible," I grumbled.

"It takes practice," Jess replied. He stepped behind me and took my wrist in his own. His chin was sandpapery with the beginnings of a beard, and it brushed my temple lightly. I felt pinpricks rippling up and down my watery spine. If I was ready to faint, surely he felt *something*?

"Turn your wrist sideways," he went on. I noticed that his voice was slightly husky. "No, more. Good. Now, when you throw the stone, keep your arm low and parallel to the water. Don't aim down, that's your whole problem."

That wasn't true. My whole problem was my central nervous system, which was having an attack of Jess Calahan. I tried to keep my muscles steady as Jess pulled my arm back and helped me toss the stone over the water. It skipped twice.

"See?" He let go of my wrist and took a giant step backward. "Nothing to it. A little practice and you'll be able to beat Mike."

"We've only got two more days," I said softly. I turned to face him, nervously twisting a strand of hair around my finger. "Not much time to practice."

"No."

Silence. I felt a cold droplet of water hit my cheek. I looked up at the sky, surprised to see that it was starless. Funny charcoal-colored clouds floated across the moon like a dirty sheet, dimming the light.

"It's going to storm," I said. "Mike was right."

"Mike's always right. I think he was born about a hundred years too late. He should have been a mountain man, like Jeremiah Johnson."

"Who?" I asked curiously.

The corners of his mouth lifted slightly. It was almost a smile. "Jeremiah Johnson was a trapper, kind of a hermit. He lived in the wilderness and fought Indians, ate bears, all that good stuff."

"Did Mike tell you what we saw today?" I asked suddenly. "I thought it was a deer, but it was bigger than a horse, and it had these enormous brown eyes . . . Jess, we saw a bull elk! It was the most beautiful thing I'd ever seen."

"You're kidding," Jess breathed. "I've never seen an elk around these parts. I thought they were all farther up in the high country."

"Well, they're not. At least, not all of them. I wish now that I'd taken a picture, but I was so excited, I never thought about it. I guess it doesn't matter, though, because I'm never going to forget that sight. And, Jess, he had these gigantic horns—"

"Antlers."

"Antlers. And they were so big, I didn't know how he could hold his head up under the weight. I wish you could have seen him."

"So do I."

For a moment we stood there, smiling at each other, and I thought, It's going to be all right. Then that blank mask slid over his face again, and the moment was gone.

"It's raining," he said. "It looks like it's going to be quite a storm. You'd better get back to your tent."

I blinked away the raindrops on my lashes. "Jess—"

Just then Mike came walking down the knoll, his hat pulled low against the rain and his plaid sleeping bag hoisted over his shoulder. I wanted to stamp my feet with frustration.

"You'd better hightail it back to your tent," he told me. "It's going to get real mean out here tonight. Jess, did you move the gals' tent away from the trees?"

"Yes. They're fine now."

"I don't get it," I said. "What's the big deal about the trees? It seems to me—"

"Lightning strikes trees," Mike interrupted. "I don't want to wake up in the morning and find two of my river rats fried. Bad for business. Now hustle on back to your tent. The wind's starting to rise, so don't forget to tie your flaps securely."

"I see." I shivered and glanced up at the sky. "Well, good night, Mike. Thanks for the lesson, Jess."

"Anytime."

And that seemed to be that. I'd wasted twenty minutes throwing rocks into the blasted river and hadn't made any progress with Jess at all. I stumbled across the beach in the darkness and crawled into our pup tent on all fours. It was aptly named, I decided sourly. It would be far more comfortable for dogs than it was for humans.

"How did it go?" Sandy asked. She was scrunched up on her sleeping bag, rolling foam-rubber curlers into her hair by flashlight.

"Wonderful. Just wonderful. I learned to skip rocks. I found out that we're going to have a mean one tonight and that fried campers are bad for business. Lightning strikes trees, so we have to tie our flaps securely and wedge the tent pegs against the polecats so that the pups stay dry."

Sandy sat up very slowly, shining the flashlight full in my face. "What did you say?"

"Nothing." I sighed. "Just go to sleep."

Chapter 7

Waiting out a thunderstorm in a pup tent on a sandbar was not my idea of fun. The steady drizzle that fell all night wasn't so bad. I slept through most of it, feeling almost cozy in my bug-green tent. But around dawn we were awakened by a wind that seemed to come from nowhere. It didn't start out as a mild whistling and then work its way up to a howl. It simply exploded around us like a hurricane someone had switched on. Next came the thunder and lightning. I would have sworn that every thunderclap was directly above our heads and that every lightning bolt was aimed at our tent pegs. The walls of our tent rippled and bulged and buckled. Sheets of rain were coming in sideways through the front opening—sideways, I swear. And no matter how many times we retied the tent flaps, the rain kept coming in.

The storm lasted only an hour or so, but it seemed much longer. When all the soggy little river rats ventured out of their tents, the sandbar was a mud pie and the beach was littered with debris. There was no dry wood for a fire, so breakfast consisted of cold cereal eaten from paper bowls.

I had Cocoa Krispies that tasted like cocoa cardboard, washed down with—what else?—Tang.

With a meaningful dirty look in Ranger's direction, I resumed my old seat in Jess's boat. If Jess noticed my little maneuver, he didn't say anything. He had his hands full at that moment helping a tearful Zack (or was it Chris?) search the beach for a compass he had dropped. By the time they found the compass, Mike's raft was already five minutes ahead of us on the river. Jess wasted no time paddling us into the strongest part of the current. It was a hard and fast rule on these expeditions that both boats were to stay in sight of one another at all times. Although we could still see Mike's raft, it was only a small brown blur in the distance that kept appearing and disappearing in the low-lying mist.

At breakfast Mike had predicted that the sun would soon dispel the fog, and we would all get a good sunburn to show for our last full day on the water. I hoped he was right. The sheer cliff walls that cut off our escape from the river were frightening enough. Rising out of the mist, they looked positively spooky. The only sounds in the world were our own voices, bouncing back to us from the fog. I missed hearing the birds calling to each other across the gorge and the comforting rustle of the aspen trees along the riverbank. I even missed the sound of Mike's harmonica.

Jess treated me like everyone else—one of the boys, a "good scout." It would have made me very depressed if I hadn't caught him staring at me while I was talking to Cameron. It was not the sort of look he would have given a "pal." It wasn't much, but at that point I needed all the encouragement I could get. If he had singled me out long enough to push me into the Colorado, I would have taken it as a good sign.

Cameron was up to new tricks. He won fifteen cents

from Chris in a game of Twenty-one, then begged me for a game of poker. I told him to find himself another patsy and settled back on my duffel bag for a midmorning nap.

I don't know exactly how it happened. I was dozing on and off, listening to snatches of conversation and sneaking drowsy looks at Jess. An hour could have passed, or only ten minutes. Suddenly I heard a high-pitched squeal and a loud splash. *Porky the pig,* I thought dreamily. *Someone has pushed Porky the Pig overboard.*

"Serves you right, Cameron," somebody said, giggling. "Anyone who cheats at cards deserves to be pushed in!"

So Cameron had gotten his just desserts. I smiled and forced my heavy eyes open. This I had to see.

And then I remembered. His life jacket. He had unfastened it to slip Chris's fifteen cents in his pocket— and he hadn't done it up again. I jumped to my feet, nearly falling overboard myself as I scanned the river for Cameron. I saw his head break water several yards behind the boat, and my worst fears were confirmed. His life jacket was floating around his shoulders like a scarf, its white straps trailing behind.

I opened my mouth to scream at Jess, but he was already shouldering past the other boys. His face was grim. He jumped up on the pontoon and dove into the water in one smooth motion. Within seconds he had Cameron safely back to the boat and was hoisting the terrified little boy high enough in the air for Chris and me to grab him by the wrists and pull him over the pontoon. Cameron was sniffing and rubbing his eyes, trying desperately not to cry. The other boys clustered around him on the raft, and I turned back to help Jess back in.

He was gone.

I blinked and looked again. Water—as far as I could see. Debris from the storm, enormous pieces of driftwood that looked like alligators slipping through the waves. And then a hand closed over the pontoon to my right. I screamed. The knuckles were raw and bloody, and even as I watched, the hand slid back into the water.

The pontoon buckled dangerously as I threw myself over it. Jess was lying facedown in the water, arms outstretched on either side. I grabbed hold of his life jacket with both hands and pulled for all I was worth. I wasn't worth much. I barely managed to keep his head above water, and the current was fighting my hold on the life jacket.

Jess's head suddenly reared back and his eyes flew open. There was a horrible purplish swelling on his forehead, and his face was paper-white. He coughed up Colorado, and his hand closed over my wrist in a death grip. I tried once more to heave him over the pontoon, this time with Chris and Zack helping.

"Not here," Jess choked out. "The boat will capsize. Pull me in from the back."

I helped him slide around the raft, keeping my hold on his life jacket while he moved, hand over hand, along the pontoon. I was terrified he would pass out again before we got him back in the boat. It would be impossible to pull him out of the water without his help. Even if I jumped in and tried to lift him as he had Cameron, I knew I wasn't strong enough to get him over the rim of the pontoon.

With Chris and Zack holding one arm and me holding the other, Jess managed to heave his chest onto the rim. He lay there for a moment, then rolled clumsily over the pontoon and onto the floor of the raft. His head lolled drunkenly from side to side, and his breathing was a hoarse rattle in his throat. Cameron started to cry, and I heard my own voice telling him that crying wouldn't help anyone.

I took off my sweater and rolled it into a ball, placing it gently beneath Jess's head. His eyes focused dazedly on me, and he tried to smile.

"It snuck up on me," he said quite clearly. "This great big rock—"

"Don't talk. Just stay quiet." In all the books I had ever read and all the movies I had seen, that was what the heroine always told the wounded hero. It seemed to do the trick. Jess closed his eyes, and his breathing evened out to a slow, steady rhythm.

Chris silently handed me a small green box. On the front in bold black letters was printed FIRST AID. I rummaged through the box until I found a small bottle of antiseptic. I dabbed it on Jess's knuckles, and his eyes flew open again.

"What the heck is that? It hurts!"

"Iodine," I said. "Don't be a coward. The Boy Scouts of America are watching you."

The four pale little faces broke into delighted smiles as Jess winked at them. It seemed to be all the reassurance they needed that he would be all right. Looking at the size of the lump on his forehead, I only wished I could be as certain.

Very gently I probed the bruised flesh. "Does that hurt?"

"Yes. When you poke at it like that, it hurts."

I strangled the sob in my throat, determined not to cry. "Don't be difficult," I managed huskily. "You just scared me—all of us—half to death. Let me look at your eyes."

Jess sighed and opened his eyes wide. I looked from one pupil to the other and frowned.

"What?" he asked with a weak grin. "No concussion?"

"Oh, Jess, I don't know. Your pupils aren't dilated or anything. I just wish I knew more about head injuries. I mean, your head looks absolutely gross. Really *awful*. You might have internal bleeding or something."

"Thank you. I feel better already." Jess propped himself up on his elbows, staring straight ahead with glazed eyes. "At least I will when everything stops spinning. Chris, can you see Mike's boat?"

Chris scrambled up the mound of supplies. "No. I can't see anything. The fog's too thick. It looks like it might rain again."

"That's okay. That's okay." Jess seemed to be talking to himself. "The current's slow . . . no more rapids. Just watch out for . . ." He scowled, as if trying to remember. "Debris. Debris from the storm. Logs and branches. Mike will probably pull over downstream to wait for us as soon as we're out of the gorge."

"Jess!"

It was Cameron, and there was a note in his voice that made my head swivel toward him and the breath catch in my throat. Now what? A tidal wave, a fire on board, a shark fin circling us in the water? What else could possibly go wrong?

Cameron was alone in the U-shaped front section of the boat, his eyes riveted on his feet. "The raft is leaking," he said.

I decided to postpone fainting. Jess literally crawled to the front of the boat after telling everyone else to stay where they were. I took one look at his face—talk about cream cheese—and followed him.

Cameron was standing in several inches of water. "Over there," he said in a tiny voice. "I think it's coming in under the pontoon."

Jess told Cameron to get in the back of the raft. He then pulled what looked like a bicycle tire pump from a duffel bag and began pumping out the boat. After about two minutes he started swaying sideways and I took over.

Soon I had pumped most of the water out of the boat. I was able to work as fast as the water came in, so I figured we were all right. For the time being.

"I'm keeping up with it," I told Jess breathlessly. "The puncture can't be too bad."

"Not yet." Jess shook his head, then winced, as if the

movement had hurt him. "Must have been the storm. Somehow the boat was damaged. . . ."

"We'll be all right." This bit of cheer was for the benefit of our frightened audience. I threw a confident little smile over my shoulder at Cameron and got absolutely no response. I went back to my pumping. "I mean, the leak isn't getting any worse. We'll just keep our handy-dandy pump going until we catch up with Mike. No problem."

"We could try," Jess said. "But we aren't going to. There's a lot of pressure on that leak, Chelsea, and there's some chance it could split wide-open. We'll have to get off the water."

For a moment I wondered if the blow to his head had affected his memory. "Jess . . ." I gestured helplessly at the cliffs surrounding us. "Where do you think we're going to beach the raft around here?"

"We're almost out of the gorge. There's a small beach about a mile downriver. Mike may even have pulled over there to wait for us. We'll make for that." Jess held my eyes with his own, passing a silent, unmistakable message. He wasn't sure the raft would make it another mile. Even now the water seemed to be coming in faster than the pump could take it out. The raft was lurching forward, like a race car with the rear end jacked up.

All things considered, I would have preferred a shark.

I paddled. I paddled until my arms were on fire and my fingers were numb. Jess tried weakly to take the paddle from me, and I told him to sit down and stop being an idiot. Terror, I discovered, made me very irritable.

Cameron pumped like a demon while we skirted the cliffs. When he got tired, Chris took over. Between the two of them they managed to keep most of the water out of the raft. I hoped there was a medal given to scouts for extreme bravery under hazardous circumstances. They deserved it. And if there was a medal for paddling under pressure, I deserved it.

It was Jess, our bleary-eyed hero of the day, who finally spotted the beach through the mist. The towering cliffs slipped back just far enough to allow for a narrow stretch of rocky shoreline. There were no trees in sight, no friendly flowers, no shelter from the rain that threatened to begin at any moment. It was the most beautiful beach I had ever seen in my life.

The scouts sent up a cheer that echoed straight to the sky. They jumped up and down on the crippled boat, slapping each other's hands and shouting. "Gimme five! Gimme five on that!"

I started to cry because I was happy and relieved, and I had just been scared half out of my wits. Jess looked at me and I smiled, but the tears kept coming.

He held out his poor battered hand, palm up. "Gimme five on that, princess."

My hero. He led our little troop across the rocky beach, promising shelter from the misty rain. His forehead bloomed with color, his eyes were glassy, and he fluttered with every breeze like a sheet hung out to dry. I supported him with one hand around his waist, and we staggered over the ground in an exhausting zigzag pattern of stop-and-go. I kept expecting him to pass out, particularly when I crunched his toes against a rock. But like the true hero he was, he kept moving. Not always forward but moving. I kept muttering encouraging little phrases such as, "You can do it" and "Just a little farther," even though I had no idea where we were headed. I made him laugh once or twice, and I thought it was probably a good sign. Surely he couldn't be hurt too badly if he could still laugh like that?

As we neared the cliff face I could see that there was a cave carved into its base. There were other caves above that, caves of all shapes and sizes that dotted the entire cliff from top to bottom. It looked like an enormous piece of mud-colored Swiss cheese.

"We stayed here once," Jess said in a tired, slurred voice. "Mike and me, when we came down the Colorado in kayaks. It'll keep us dry till help comes."

The cave was shallow, and the watery gray sun provided sufficient light to see from one end to the other. It was perhaps forty feet wide, giving us more than enough room for everyone to roll out a sleeping bag if—heaven forbid—we had to spend the night. There was a circle of charred rocks in one corner, as well as a small pile of dry wood. The floor of the cave was littered with beer and soda-pop cans, which I found very comforting. If littering was a problem here, we couldn't be too far off the beaten track.

Jess sank weakly down on the dusty ground, resting his head against the wall of the cave. Eyes closed, shoulders slumped, he was silent while the scouts carried in the duffel bags from the boat. The boys were having the time of their lives now that the immediate danger was past. They discussed wilderness survival, the best way to trap squirrels and chipmunks, and which plants and roots were edible. A lively argument broke out as to the actual food value of earthworms.

Although I doubted very much that food was going to be a problem, I didn't dampen the boys' enthusiasm for their adventure by saying so. Still in the raft was a cooler full of perishables, plus the box lunches that had been passed out that morning and several six-packs of Shasta. Not to mention the year's supply of candy Cameron carried in his duffel bag.

I knelt down beside Jess and touched his shoulder gently. "I'm going to get the rest of the supplies from the boat. I'll be right back."

"I'll go with you." He started to get up, his eyes still closed.

"No, you won't." I placed both hands on his shoulders and gently pushed him back down again. "You're exhausted. You've probably got a blazing headache too. Just go back to sleep."

"I'm not sleeping," he muttered. "I'm just resting."

"Then rest. I'll be right back."

I was nearly out of the cave when he called me.

"Chelsea?"

"Yes?" I hurried over and knelt down again beside him. "What is it? Your head?"

"No. Look, there's a yellow flag in the boat in a plastic bag. It's a distress flag. Tie it to the raft where it can be seen from the water, will you?"

"Sure." I stood up. "Don't worry about a thing."

"Chelsea?"

I stopped dead in my tracks. If Jess wasn't injured, this might get a little irritating. "Yes?"

"Take Ryan with you. You'll need some help with the cooler."

"All right."

"Chelsea?"

"*What*?"

"You're beautiful when you're bugged."

He winked at me with an eye that was rapidly turning black and blue. My irritation evaporated like steam. I wondered how I ever could have admired the dark good looks of Gary Quinn. There was something infinitely more appealing about a boy with dripping blond hair and a lump on his forehead the size of a grapefruit.

By the time Ryan and I returned, the rain was falling in sheets. Our shoes were enormous blocks of mud, and our clothes dripped pools on the floor of the cave. Ryan— lucky little boy that he was—changed into a dry set of clothes in front of all. The mind of a ten-year-old was a wonderful thing. I wasn't quite so uninhibited. I had to content myself with an extra sweater and a brisk rubdown with a towel.

Jess was stretched out on a sleeping bag, his eyes closed

and his chest rising and dropping with the deep, even rhythm of sleep. He was oblivious to the arm wrestling taking place in the corner, and he didn't even twitch when the winner let loose with a victory yell. Everyone began complaining about their empty stomachs, so I located the box lunches and passed them out. Each Scout devoured two sandwiches, an orange, a package of potato chips, and a box of miniature doughnuts. I figured this ought to keep them quiet until I decided what to do about dinner. There were chunks of beef and potatoes and carrots in plastic bags in the cooler. My mother the nutritionist would know what to do with them. Sandy would know what to do with them. Even my brother could probably turn out a meal without poisoning anyone. Why, oh, why had I dropped out of home ec to take theater arts? I could recite every line of the balcony scene of *Romeo and Juliet* by heart, but raw meat and vegetables threw me into a state of shock.

Jess had warned me that Mike probably wouldn't realize anything had happened to us until he pulled over to shore late that afternoon. By the time he notified the river patrol, it would be too dark to begin searching. Unless a miracle happened, we were on our own until morning. I waited by the solid curtain of rain that sealed off our cave, listening and watching for a miracle. Eventually the rain let up long enough to allow a brief, washed-out sunset. I walked back down to the beach, scanning the river in both directions. Water, water everywhere . . . and not a boat in sight. I finally faced the fact that it would be at least twelve more hours until help came. Twelve hours—or more—until Jess could receive proper medical attention. Although he seemed all right, head injuries could be far more serious than they appeared. My knowledge of first aid began and ended with putting on a Band-Aid. I was beginning to feel like the only skill I had developed in my seventeen years was the unremarkable ability to French-braid my own hair.

I went back to the cave, determined to do battle with

dinner without anyone's help. Jess was still asleep, his face turned toward the wall. Standing over him, I could see that his cheeks were flushed with sleep and his breathing regular, yet something still bothered me. Something . . .

Sleep. I might have heard it on television or in my health class, but I suddenly knew that I shouldn't let Jess sleep. If he did in fact have a concussion, it could be dangerous. I couldn't remember why exactly—it had something to do with the possibility of falling into a coma—but I did know that he shouldn't be sleeping.

I shook him gently, then with more force. I was about thirty seconds away from wild hysteria when Jess turned his head and focused on me sleepily.

"Wasamatter?" he said thickly. "Can't you find the flag?"

"The flag? What—oh, the flag. I found it, everything's fine. How's your head?"

"My head." He rolled over on his back and stared at the ceiling. "It feels like somebody is working on it with a jackhammer," he said finally. "I want my mommy."

I giggled, relieved to hear him sounding like his old self. "You'll have to make do with the assistant scoutmaster. Would you like a couple of aspirins? Or a cold drink?"

"Yes to both. Thanks."

While I rummaged in the cooler for a Coke—I thought a nice dose of caffeine might help keep Jess alert—the scouts clustered around him like an enthusiastic fan club. Was his head killing him? How had he hurt his hand? What was it like to almost drown? Did he want to play a few hands of poker? (This from Cameron.)

I shouldered my way through to the patient and told the troops to get a fire built before it got too dark to see. Immediately they began fighting about who got to light the match.

"I light the fire," I said, doing my best to sound confident. "You guys just get the wood ready."

"No need. Your fearless leader will take care of it." Jess got unsteadily to his feet, still holding the can of Coke. I watched the blood drain from his face, as if someone had pulled a plug in his heel. "Good as new," he said. I caught him as he pitched forward, getting a face full of Coke for my efforts. "Damn. Sorry, Chelsea." He leaned heavily on me for a moment, then straightened slowly. "Lost my balance for a minute there. I'm just a little . . . dizzy. Sorry."

"It's all right." I wiped at the Coke drizzling down my chin with one hand and supported Jess around the waist with the other. "Look, why don't you be a good boy and sit down? Fearless leader or not, you're in no condition to be on your feet. I can certainly handle cooking dinner. I'm not entirely helpless." I hoped.

Jess didn't argue, which showed that he was either still in shock or in a great deal of pain. He slumped back down against the wall, draining the last of the Coke in one gulp. "I feel like an idiot," he muttered.

Cameron needed no further encouragement. He was beside Jess in a flash, dealing out cards on the dusty floor. When Jess protested that he was still seeing double, Cameron grinned and upped the ante. Looking at Jess's ashen face and his drawn mouth, my first instinct was to tell Cameron to leave him alone and let him rest. Then I realized that a poker game would be just the thing to keep Jess awake while I fixed dinner. In his condition he would probably lose his shirt, but at least I wouldn't have to worry about him slipping into a coma.

The fire was a cinch. The boys knew exactly how to lay the wood and tinder, courtesy of Tracy Wigwam Scout Camp. I only used up half a book of matches getting the thing lit, which was a great improvement over my first attempt at Chicken Cliff. As soon as the blaze was going strong Zack entertained Chris and Ryan with finger shadows on the wall of the cave. No one seemed to have the slightest interest in what I was going to do to their dinner—what I was going to *fix* for their dinner—which suited me just fine.

I was a whiz with a microwave. I could make wonderful things with ice cream in a blender, and I was famous at home for my blueberry waffles. But I didn't have a microwave or a blender or a Teflon-coated waffle iron. I had a fire and several plastic bags full of meat and vegetables. I also had a cast-iron cooking pot and a small grill that would support it over the fire. It didn't seem like much.

I suddenly had a stroke of brilliance. Mulligan Hash. Whenever my father got the rare urge to cook, he always made Mulligan Hash. That was a fancy name for throwing whatever leftovers happened to be in the refrigerator into a pot and letting them simmer into a thick gook. One of my father's favorite sayings was that he had never met a Mulligan Hash he didn't like. Surprisingly enough, neither had I.

Into the pot went the meat and vegetables. I found a can of tomato juice in the cooler and poured it over the vegetables. Then I really got into the spirit of the thing and added a package of beef jerky, some leftover cheese slices, two withered hot dogs, and a can of chili con carne. I stirred the whole concoction over the fire until it looked like very lumpy red oatmeal and my eyebrows were singed from the heat.

There was some hesitation at first when everyone sat down to eat. Cameron whispered something about food poisoning, but Jess quieted him with a grim look. And then, as fearless leaders should, he dug in his spoon and took the first bite.

"It's good." He looked at me with something like wonder in his expression. "Chelsea, it's really *good.*"

They all had seconds. I felt as if I had been awarded the Nobel Prize or something. And no one made gagging and choking noises the way Ranger always did when he ate something I had fixed. For the rest of the night I went around with a goofy, lopsided smile on my face, amazed that a simple pot of Mulligan Hash could do so much for my self-esteem.

The rain continued providing a glistening, moonlit curtain for our cave. Eventually the humidity and the heat from the fire put our little troop asleep one by one. Cameron was the last to go. He nodded off in a tight little ball on the floor, his head pillowed on one of my damp sweaters. Jess managed to carry him to his sleeping bag without staggering, but when he returned, his jaw seemed rigid, as if he were clenching against the pain in his head. I wanted to help him, somehow wave a magic wand and ease his suffering. All I could do was offer him another couple of aspirins and try not to stare at the grotesque swelling on his head. And somehow I had to keep him awake.

"Listen," Jess said tiredly. "Do you know what that sound is?"

We were sitting on our sleeping bags watching the fire die down to a flickering orange glow. I glanced nervously at the void beyond the cave. I could hear nothing but the river and the rain. "No," I whispered. "What?"

"Silence. Peace. Quiet. I was just about ready to gag these guys with their own life jackets. This is like being in solitary confinement with a circus."

"It's the cave." I smiled, relieved to know that I wouldn't be battling any wild boars that night. "Everything echoes in here, doesn't it? I'll bet it doesn't do your headache much good."

Jess yawned, and I could see that even that small movement caused him discomfort. "It's easing up a little. Matter of fact, I think I'll try and get some shut-eye myself. If I know Mike, he'll have the river patrol out looking for us at the crack of dawn. It shouldn't take them long to find us here."

"I thought we might have a game of cards," I said quickly. It was the first thing that came to mind.

Jess gave me a strange look. "Cards? Don't tell me I've got another cardsharp on my hands. Cameron's already taken me for everything but my gold fillings."

"Well, not exactly." I squirmed. "I was thinking of maybe . . . Fish or something. I never really learned how to play poker."

Jess cracked the first smile I had seen in hours. "Fish? As in the game of Fish? As in "give me all of your sixes?""

"Well, it's the only card game I know how to play. Except Concentration," I added hopefully. "Do you know how to play Concentration? You spread all the cards out on the floor and then try to—"

"I know how to play Concentration," Jess interrupted. "I also know how to play Fish. Now ask me if I'm going to."

"Are you?"

"No. I've played cards tonight until I'm blue in the face. I'm going to sleep while the going's good." He stretched out on his sleeping bag and gave me an absentminded pat on my stockinged foot. "Night, princess."

"The fire's going out," I said desperately.

"Good. This cave is like an oven."

"But I'm cold," I insisted. "I'm freezing and there's no more wood."

Jess peered at me through a heavy veil of lashes. "You're sweating."

"I'm cold, I really am! We need to find some more wood so that we can keep the fire going." I stressed the *we*.

Jess made a sound that was more of a groan than a sigh. He levered himself into a sitting position and looked at me squarely. "Number one," he said. "It's raining outside. There is no dry wood to be found. Number two, if you're really cold, why don't you get into your sleeping bag instead of sitting there on top of it? And number three, if you aren't sweating, I'm a duckbill platypus.''

We had a staring contest. I looked away first.

"Aha! Just as I thought," Jess said triumphantly. "Nurse Chelsea is at it again. Are you still worried about a concussion? I promise you, I'm not going to slip into a coma if I fall asleep. That's what you're afraid of, isn't it?"

I shrugged and scratched a mosquito bite on my arm.

"Chelsea, your imagination is working overtime. All I need is a good night's rest and I'll be fine. I don't have a concussion, cross my heart."

"How do you know?" I demanded. "Admit it, Jess. You could have a concussion, and if you do, you shouldn't sleep for the first twelve hours." I had no idea if twelve hours was the prescribed time limit, but I wanted to sound knowledgeable.

"I could have a concussion," Jess said patiently. "But I don't, and I'm tired and I'm going to sleep. End of discussion. Now close your baby blues and get some rest."

I had perfected one other skill besides French-braiding my hair and reciting *Romeo and Juliet*. I decided that now might be an excellent time to use it. I looked at Jess, and my eyes filled with tears, huge heartbreaking alligator tears that rolled silently down my cheeks. My drama coach at school had always been very impressed with my ability to cry on cue.

"Oh, for Pete's sake, don't cry," Jess said uncomfortably. "Chelsea, I can't stand it when girls do that. All right already. I'll stay awake, I promise. I'll stand on my head and stack jelly beans with my eyebrows, but *stop crying.*"

We played Fish. We played Concentration. We ate the last of the Mulligan Hash and stole some of the licorice Cameron had won from Jess. The fire died, and we lit a Coleman lantern, and Jess taught me how to tie knots in a piece of twine. I learned to make a square knot and a granny knot, but I couldn't get the hang of the barrel knot, which Jess told me every good fisherman should know.

"Why?" I asked crossly, trying to untangle the mess I had made of the twine. "You can't tell me that fish care how the line is tied."

"Oh, but they do." Jess looked at me solemnly. "You use this knot to connect the two leaders together. Once the knot is tied—correctly, not in a wad like that—it looks sort of like a torpedo. Since the ends can be trimmed very close, it causes very little disturbance in the water. That way you don't frighten the fish."

"By all means, we mustn't frighten the fish. We're going to catch them and skin them and eat them, but we wouldn't want to frighten them." Jess doubled over with laughter, and I threw the snarl of twine at his head. "Tie it yourself, you fish murderer. What's a leader, anyway?"

"A leader connects the fishhook or the lure with the—"

"No. Don't tell me. If I learn any more about fishing, I might actually have to go one day."

We talked all through the slow-motion hours of the night. My eyes grew red and gritty, and Jess punctuated every sentence with a yawn, but we managed to stay awake. Jess asked me the simple, everyday questions no other boy had ever thought to ask. What was my favorite color? Did I like to sleep late on weekends or get up early? Did I like Chinese food, parades, reading the Sunday comics? What was my favorite holiday? Did I have a pet, and why the devil would anyone want to own a *canary*?

In turn I discovered that Jess Calahan wasn't named after a mountain man as I had thought, but after his mother's favorite uncle. His middle name was Alexander, and he was born on Christmas Day. He was allergic to peanuts and had once broken his leg in three places falling out of a tree house. He wanted to be a biologist someday and would be attending the University of Colorado in

September. He had a German shepherd named Mickey, who was brave, loyal, and devoted, and ate twiddling little canaries for breakfast.

I don't remember when the rain finally stopped. I looked beyond the cave and suddenly saw the earth and sky separating into two distinct colors. Within minutes the sky was more blue than black, and the moisture was rising in wispy spirals from the damp earth.

"The storm's passed," I said quietly. "It shouldn't be too long now before help comes."

And then I looked at Jess Alexander Calahan and burst into tears. Real tears.

"Chelsea?"

I sniffed noisily and looked away. Jess sighed and gathered me awkwardly into his arms, patting my back as if I were a baby that needed to be burped.

"Here we go again," he said resignedly. "I swear, princess, you are the wettest girl I've ever met. Every time I look at you, your nose is running."

"I'm not that bad," I said, quavering.

"No. No, you're not." He drew back, cradling my head between his hands. "I was only trying to make you smile. Chelsea, I don't know what I would have done without you for the last twenty-four hours. After I was hurt you took over like a real pro, and I know it wasn't easy for you. Believe me, no one deserves a good cry more than you do."

"That's not it."

He brushed a tear from my cheek with his thumb. "Then what is it?"

"I don't know!" And I didn't, not really. It had something to do with Jess's rainbow-colored eye and his bruised forehead and the fact that he was going to be all right. I couldn't explain it any more than I could explain why a part of me didn't want the sun to rise that morning. I *wanted* to go home. I wanted to sleep in my white lace canopy bed. I wanted to curl up on my window seat and talk on the telephone for hours. And I wanted Jess to see me in a dress, with my hair curled and my makeup perfect.

Why, then, the tears?

"Maybe you just want to go home, princess." There was an odd, pinched look on Jess's face, as if he were in pain again.

"Maybe." I managed a smile between the hiccups I always got when I cried. "Is your head hurting again? I think it would be safe now for you to sleep."

"No time," he said quietly. He bent his head, and his mouth moved over mine, his lips clinging for the barest, sweetest second. "I wish . . ."

"What?" My voice was a faint whisper. My hiccups were suddenly cured, which came as no great surprise. A kiss that could curl my toes should certainly be able to cure hiccups.

"Nothing." He drew an unsteady breath. "We'd better wake up the boys. I have a feeling we're about to be rescued."

It was only then that I became aware of the sounds from the beach. Footsteps grating on rock, murmuring voices. Men's voices. I thought I heard Jess sigh, but it might have been the wind.

"Up here," someone yelled. "Check the cave."

Chapter 8

The river behaved itself beautifully all the way to Kelly's Crossing. No submerged boulders, no white water, no whirlpools. Just a winding ribbon of water that whispered sweet nothings in the breeze. More than once the Colorado had shown us who was boss. Now it seemed content to let us enjoy our last few hours on the river in peace. The weather also cooperated very nicely. The thunderclouds had dissipated into drifting, cotton-puff swirls in a soft blue sky. The air was warm and scented with rain-washed freshness. Mother Nature had already played every trick in the book on us. I guess she figured enough was enough.

Our two rescuers were members of the Colorado Search and Rescue Team. Apparently Mike had contacted them by radio the evening before, when he first realized we were missing. He remembered the cave where he and Jess had once camped overnight and suggested they check it, which was how they found us so quickly.

The Search and Rescue boat made our little raft look like a water balloon. It was an enormous craft that seemed to be a cross between Cleopatra's barge and a gas-powered picnic table. It had four redwood benches lashed between

two giant pontoons and a small outboard motor at the
rear. There was more than enough room for eight of us
and all of our supplies. Cameron and his friends were
ecstatic riding in an official rescue vehicle. I could see that
it was the high point of the entire trip for them, even better
than being stranded overnight. If only they could have
been carried out of the cave on a stretcher like Jess. It
would have put the finishing touches on a grand
adventure.

Jess was quickly examined by a member of the rescue
team. He advised Jess to see a doctor as soon as he got
home, but he didn't think there should be any complica-
tions. If indeed Jess had suffered a concussion, we had
done the right thing by keeping him awake during the
night.

"See, Chelsea?" Jess gave me a rakish grin. "I told you
I wasn't supposed to sleep."

I stuck out my tongue and threw a half-eaten plum at
him.

Originally we had been scheduled to arrive by noon at
Kelly's Crossing, where our trip would officially end. Jess
explained that this was a small, parklike area that boasted
a gas station, public rest rooms, and an access road to the
freeway. Here another employee of Calahan Expeditions
would be waiting with the van to transport us home.
Although we were now a couple of hours behind schedule,
we would probably be back in Denver by dinnertime.

I was surprised that this news didn't make me happier. I
was going to be home for dinner. Mom would probably
outdo herself preparing a welcome-home feast. I could
take a bubble bath and give my poor hair a hot oil treat-
ment. I could wash the grit from my feet once and for all
and put on my fluffy pink bunny slippers. Eden.

Yet I was conscious of a strange reluctance to put an end
to my adventures. All things considered, I hadn't made
such a bad river rat. I trailed my fingers through the cold

water of the mighty Colorado and smiled to myself. I had waged a private war with this moody river for five days. I had been shipwrecked, drenched, and nearly drowned, but I was still here. Surely that counted for something?

"Admit it," I whispered to the murky depths. "Chelsea Anne Hyatt is tougher than she looks."

"What did you say?" Jess asked.

"Nothing." I looked at the sun-browned face of the boy beside me, at the bright tangle of wind-tossed hair, and thought: *I must remember this as long as I live.*

It was over before I knew it. We rounded a bend in the river and sailed straight into civilization. There was a gas station with a neon sign that dwarfed the pine trees, a smoothly manicured lawn that stretched down to the beach, and a small concrete building that I assumed housed the rest rooms. I could also see the metallic-gray glint of the Calahan Expeditions van in the parking lot behind the gas station.

The Search and Rescue team had radioed ahead to Mike as soon as they found us. We had a welcoming committee waiting on the beach, headed by a burly man in a Mickey Mouse cap and a "Save the Whales" T-shirt. Mike gave Jess a big bear hug, ruffled a few scouts heads, and kissed me on the cheek. Pretty soon everyone was kissing and hugging. Sandy was laughing and crying at the same time, and even Ranger looked suspiciously bright-eyed. For the first time since our kindergarten days he gave me a swift hug.

"Idiot," he said. "What was the big idea, scaring us all like that?"

"I thought it would make you appreciate me," I said cheerfully. "But if you're still calling me an idiot, it didn't work."

"Oh, yes, it did." Sandy paused to blow her nose loudly into a handkerchief. "You should have seen him last night when we realized you were missing. He paced the beach all night long, shining his little flashlight over the water. I couldn't even get him to sit down until he heard you were all right."

I looked at Ranger, and he looked away, two spots of color burning high in his cheeks. "I'd better go help load the trailer," he muttered.

"Wait a minute." Sandy sniffed and smiled, holding out the sodden handkerchief. "You can have this back now. Thanks."

Ranger backed away, grimacing. "You keep it. Please. Think of it as a present from me to you."

Jess was under strict orders from his uncle to rest while everyone else loaded the trailer. He reclined in the shade of an old cottonwood tree, grinning and waving while we lugged duffel bags up the grassy incline. As soon as the supplies were loaded Sandy and I made a beeline for the rest rooms. It was the first time in five days we had had access to indoor plumbing, a convenience I would never take for granted again. There was nothing like a camping trip to make you appreciate the little things in life.

It was also the first opportunity I had had to look into a mirror. I stared at my reflection, rubbed my eyes, and looked again. My hair was dead straight, almost white from the burn of the water and the sun. My eyes looked pale and colorless against my sunburned face, and my normally high, slanted cheekbones had disappeared in a rash of lumpy mosquito bites. My clothes were filthy, and in the close confines of the rest room, I realized that they had a personality of their own. Although I'd never gotten close enough to a squirrel to smell it, I imagined it would smell something like me.

Sandy's expression was no less disgusted than my own. "*Now* I know why Ranger kissed me," she said. "I look like one of those wild forest creatures he's so crazy about."

I ran my fingers through my hair, trying to plump it up a

bit. It responded with all the bounce and shine of brittle straw. "Have you got a comb?"

"Nope. Everything's in my duffel bag. Where's your Vaseline?"

I sighed. "Duffel bag."

In the end we had to content ourselves with washing our hands and faces. Everyone else was already in the van when we returned to the parking lot. Jess was in the front seat between Mike and the new driver, fast asleep. Ranger was in the back, also dead to the world. Sandy and I wedged ourselves in beside him, tripping over the long legs that seemed to be everywhere.

"I can tell already," Sandy said in a low voice. "We aren't going to get much conversation out of Rip Van Winkle here. I stepped on his foot and he didn't even twitch. Oh, well. At least you and I can talk."

I yawned, watching Kelly's Crossing disappear into the distance. "Sure."

"I want to know everything. *Everything,* from the beginning to the end. It sounds so romantic—you and Jess, stranded together—"

"With four Boy Scouts," I interrupted sleepily.

"A minor detail. Now tell me, how did it happen? I mean, I know the boat sprung a leak, but how did you feel? Did you panic? And poor Jess, his face looks like a Halloween mask. Don't you think a guy looks cute with a black eye? I mean, Jess is good-looking, anyway, but *wounded* he's adorable. Don't you think?"

I wanted to tell her that Jess hadn't felt so adorable during our long night in the cave. I wanted to explain how he had carried Cameron so gently to his sleeping bag and never complained once about the pain. And I wanted to tell her that I would never care about anyone the way I cared about Jess Alexander Calahan, born on Christmas Day and named after his favorite uncle.

But my eyelids were weighted down with exhaustion,

and the sun outside my window was far too bright. I leaned back tiredly against the seat and hoped that Sandy would forgive me for postponing our conversation because I had a sneaking suspicion that the snoring I heard was my own.

I woke up once—briefly—when we stopped for gas on the road. I didn't come to again until the van pulled to a halt in front of the red-brick office building where our trip had begun. My first thought was gratitude that I had made it home in one piece. My second thought was that every part of me ached, courtesy of a four-hour nap in a very cramped position.

I stumbled out of the van like a sleepwalker and adjusted red eyes to a sunset that was smeared with gray city haze. Only this morning I had felt like an orphan in the wilderness, totally cut off from civilization. Now I stood on an acre of black asphalt, directly across the street from a McDonalds, a Burger King and a First Interstate Bank with a twenty-four-hour automated teller. The whole thing had a sense of unreality about it.

The parking lot was a beehive of activity for the next twenty minutes. Scouts were whisked away one by one until only Cameron was still waiting for his parents. I noticed Jess and Ranger whispering together, and then Ranger approached Cameron with a mouse-eating grin that I would have recognized anywhere. Unfortunately Cameron didn't know my devious brother quite so well.

"How about a game of poker?" Ranger suggested cheerfully. "One more for the road, huh, kid?"

It was all over in a matter of minutes. Ranger took Cameron to the cleaners, and the poor kid lost everything but his scout shorts. I knew Ranger for the cardsharp he was, and I thought it was a pretty sneaky trick to fleece a little Boy Scout. I had my mouth open to tell him so when Ranger caught my eye and winked. He gathered up his winnings (which consisted mainly of candy, crinkled dollar bills, and bubble gum) and dropped everything into Cameron's lap.

"One thing my old pappy always told me," Ranger said, affecting a terrible western drawl. "It doesn't matter how good you are, boy. There is always going to be someone out there who's better."

I disguised my giggles with a sudden burst of coughing. I had heard this line innumerable times on the late-night westerns Ranger was addicted to. It sounded pure cornball to me, but Cameron was soaking it up like a sponge. I had a feeling it would be a long time before he touched another deck of cards.

Eventually only Sandy and I were left in the parking lot, yawning and watching for the headlights of my father's white Mercedes. Ranger had gone into the office to buy us drinks from the pop machine. Jess and Mike were arguing from somewhere inside the building. I couldn't hear the words, but it sounded like Jess was objecting—strongly— to being taken to the hospital for an examination.

Ranger came out of the office juggling three cans of Dr Pepper. "I don't get it," he said. "Dad should have been here thirty minutes ago. He's never late."

"He is tonight," I replied. "Look, why don't you call him again? Maybe something came up and he was delayed."

"Maybe." Ranger drained his can without taking a breath. "Man, that tasted good. You want the rest of yours?"

I looked at my unopened can. "Yeah, I think I'll have a bit more," I said sarcastically. "You don't mind, do you?"

It went right over his head. "Nah, I don't mind. What did he say when you called him?"

"Who?"

"Who do you think? Dad! Was he leaving right away or what?"

"How should I know? You're the one who talked to him!"

Sandy cleared her throat and stepped between us, assuming the position of referee. She looked at me and sighed. "Apparently Ranger is under the impression that *you* called your father to pick us up." And then she turned to Ranger and said, "Chelsea thinks *you* called your father to pick us up. Now, does everyone have a clear understanding of the situation or should I go over it again?"

"Smart aleck," I muttered. "Ranger, you were in and out of that office a hundred times helping to unload the trailer. I just assumed you would call Dad while you were in there."

"And since I was so busy," Ranger shot back, "I figured you would call him. It's not like you had anything else to do. All you've done since we got here is sit on your duff."

Sandy shrugged, looking at Ranger with wide brown eyes. "I guess I'll go call my dad. It looks like that's the only way I'm going to get home tonight."

Sandy's forlorn little voice had the most incredible effect on my obnoxious brother. Right before my very eyes he turned into Sir Lancelot.

"You stay where you are," he said firmly. "I'll take care of everything. I'll go call Dad right now, and we'll have you home in no time."

He practically sprinted into the office. I shook my head, looking at Sandy with undisguised admiration. "I am truly impressed," I said humbly. "You really do have a way with animals."

No sooner had Ranger disappeared into the building than he came back out again, followed by Mike and a sullen-looking Jess. "No problem," he said. "Mike and Jess will drop us off. They're going to St. Benedict's Hospital to have Jess examined, so it's right on their way."

I smiled sympathetically at Jess, hoping to erase the thunderclouds from his face. "You lost, huh?"

"I lost," he confirmed shortly. "No one seems to want to believe that I'm all right. I've got a feeling that I'm going to disappoint a lot of people if I don't have at least a brain tumor."

"I'll be happy with a simple concussion," I said. "Then I'll know I didn't stay up all night in vain."

"Brat," he said softly. And then he smiled, his swollen eye crinkling like dried mud. He looked like a little boy who had lost a couple of rounds with the local bully. I wanted to put my arms around him and hug him.

Mike locked up the office and ordered us into the van once again. Tweedle-Dee the Wonder Dummy (alias Ranger Hyatt) slid into the front seat with Jess and Mike, leaving Sandy and me to share the back. I noticed my friend glaring at the back of Ranger's head, and I knew she wasn't any happier with the seating arrangements than I was. Ranger had made some progress as a potential boyfriend, but he obviously had a long way to go. I had hoped to sit next to Jess during the ride home. It would have given him the perfect opportunity to say something along the lines of, "I'll call you tomorrow" or "Maybe we could catch a movie sometime." As it was, I had to be content with listening to Ranger and Mike discuss various ways of tying flies. I had visions of little flies bound and gagged before I realized that they were talking about making their own fishing lures from feathers and twine.

It took us less than twenty minutes to turn onto Country Club Drive. We dropped Sandy off at her house, then pulled into our circular driveway next door. As usual our two-story colonial was blazing with lights. My mother is a rebel when it comes to conserving electricity. She can't stand to walk past a darkened room, including the bathroom.

I waited with Jess by the van while Mike and Ranger got our bags out of the trailer. He was unusually quiet, and I wondered if his head was bothering him.

"You must be pretty tired," I said finally. "It's been a long couple of days for you."

Jess shrugged. "No more than for you. You were the nurse, I was only the patient." He met my eyes, and a reluctant smile curved his mouth. "All right, go ahead and say it."

I opened my eyes innocently. "Say what?"

"That I was a lousy patient. Poor Chelsea. You haven't had it easy this week, have you? I wish there was some way I could make it up to you."

Ask me out, you fool. "Just get well," I said lamely.

"I am well. Getting anybody to believe I'm okay is a different story." He leaned one hip against the van, then stood up straight again and pushed both hands into the pockets of his jeans. What did all of his restlessness mean? Was he that eager to leave? He began pacing the driveway, his gaze straying to the flower beds that edged the lawn. "You have a beautiful home."

"Thank you." I couldn't understand the sudden constraint between us. Perhaps Jess really was in pain or simply bone-tired. In profile his face was withdrawn, strangely guarded. When Ranger was sick or injured, he complained loudly enough for the entire neighborhood to hear. Maybe Jess was the type who kept to himself when he didn't feel well.

Mike was clearly anxious to get Jess to the hospital. He hustled him into the van and turned out of the driveway with a farewell blast on the horn. It was not an ordinary horn. Mike Calahan had a specially made device that played the entire first verse of "The Star Spangled Banner." Several porch lights went on across the street, and my father appeared in our doorway in his red velour bathrobe.

"Who's there?" he called. "Chelsea? Ranger? Is that you?"

"In person," Ranger said. "The river rats have returned."

We walked into the light spilling from the doorway. Dad looked from me to Ranger and quickly back at me. His eyes widened, and a smile was stuck on his face. "*Chelsea*?"

I nodded, chewing down the last fingernail I had left. With my other hand I scratched at a mosquito bite on my head.

Dad stared at me for a long moment. His lips twitched, and he made a funny little gurgling noise in his throat, but on the whole he showed remarkable restraint. He called to my mother inside the house with only the faintest tremor running through his voice. "Irene? Come here a moment, darling. And bring the camera, will you?"

I sat down to dinner with my hair still dripping from a quick shower. The long-awaited bubble bath had been postponed indefinitely due to hunger. Mom had prepared all of our favorites: crusty, whole-wheat rolls; spaghetti and meatballs; and fresh peach cobbler. I actually caught myself checking my water glass for flies. Being back in civilization was going to take a little getting used to.

While we ate, Ranger and I gave a brief summary of our five-day adventure. We told them about the accident that had injured Jess and left everyone in my raft stranded, trying to make it sound like more of an inconvenience than a nightmare. Judging by my mother's stricken expression and my father's threat never to let me out of his sight again, I don't think we were entirely convincing.

Halfway through the meal the telephone rang. I nearly broke my leg trying to get out of my chair to answer it, but Ranger was closer. Although I strained to hear what he was saying, he spoke in quiet monosyllables that sounded like some kind of yoga chant. When he came back to the table, he was grinning from ear to ear.

"That was Mike," he said. "He was calling from the hospital. They're sending Jess home with a clean bill of health and a sore—" he glanced at Mom—"fanny."

"Fantastic!" I sagged against my chair in relief, then frowned at my brother. "What do you mean, a sore fanny?"

"A sore sit-down," Mom corrected firmly.

Ranger and I exchanged a pained look. He dropped back into his chair, digging with gusto into a second helping of spaghetti. "Apparently Jess's hand was scraped up pretty badly," he mumbled through the food in his mouth. "They gave him a tetanus shot just to be on the safe side, right in the old—sit-down. Poor Jess couldn't get the nurse to give it to him in his arm. The *nurse*," he repeated gleefully. "Oh, wait till I see Calahan. He'll never live this one down!"

I wanted to ask Ranger when he thought he would be seeing Jess again, but I restrained myself. I didn't want to appear desperate. And Ranger was the type who wouldn't think twice about telling Jess that I *was* desperate.

Besides, maybe I was worrying about nothing. True, Jess hadn't said anything about seeing me again, but maybe that was because there had always been people around us, and he didn't like an audience when he asked a girl for a date. Or maybe he was shy. I recalled his kisses at Chicken Cliff and decided that shyness was not his problem. He was probably just waiting until his appearance improved. If I had a face the color of blueberry jam, I wouldn't want to go out with anyone, either. Patience, Chelsea Anne, patience.

Later that night I picked up the telephone in my bedroom and dialed Sandy's number. She answered after the first ring.

"Where were you!" I asked. "Sitting on the phone?"

"I sort of thought Ranger might call," she admitted sheepishly. "Just to say good night or . . . something."

I stretched out on my bed, enjoying the luxury of a smooth sleeping surface. And there wasn't an ant in sight. "Ranger didn't even tell me good night. He fell asleep watching a television documentary on wildebeasts. Dad practically had to carry him to bed. Honestly, sometimes I wonder what you see in him."

"I like a good challenge," Sandy said, sighing. "Oh, well. At least I wrangled a date out of him. We're going to a movie tomorrow night."

"And he's paying?" I asked, only half joking. "Wow, this must be serious. He's saving up for a new pair of hiking boots. It takes a crowbar to get any money out of his wallet."

"See?" Sandy giggled. "I am making progress. By the time the homecoming dance rolls around, he'll be begging me to go with him."

"Don't count on it," I warned her. "Ranger avoids dances like the plague. He won't even wear a tie, let alone a suit. As a matter of fact, I don't think he even *owns* a tie."

"Then he'll have to buy one," Sandy said firmly. "Hey, I've got a great idea. We'll double-date with you and Jess."

"And what makes you think Jess wants to go out with me?" I grabbed my pillow and hugged it, cradling the phone on my shoulder. "He sure didn't act very interested tonight. We barely exchanged two words."

"Don't be stupid. Of course he wants to go out with you. Every boy who looks at you wants to go out with you. It's one of the things I hate about you."

By the time I hung up, I was feeling more optimistic. One of the terrific things about having a best friend is that they always know exactly what to say. Perhaps I was imagining a strain between Jess and me tonight. I decided that only time would tell. I just hoped it wouldn't take too much time.

I enjoyed the feeling of padding around my room in bare feet as I went about my nightly getting-ready-for-bed ritual. No rocks to stumble over, no thorns pricking me, no snakes slithering across my path. For the first time in my life I paused to appreciate the lock on my bathroom door—so much more private than hiding behind a tree. And when I crawled into bed, I didn't have to worry about what might have crawled in before me.

My mattress was firm yet cushiony, the bedding soft and warm. And yet there were marshmallowy lumps I didn't remember, valleys I rolled into, and squeaking bedsprings that startled me whenever I moved. The flowery fabric softener Mom had used on the sheets seemed almost cloying after the sharp tang of fresh mountain air. I opened the window, but a sluggish summer breeze carried the faint odors of exhaust and a neighbor's barbecued chicken. In the distance I could hear the lonely wail of an ambulance siren.

Civilization *was* going to take a little getting used to.

Chapter 9

"Chelsea! You have a visitor!"

My mother's voice galvanized me into action. Although it was already eleven o'clock on Saturday morning, I still wasn't dressed. I had been dragging around my room the entire morning, filing what was left of my nails, sorting out the clothes I had taken on the river trip, listening with my fingers crossed for the phone to ring. It had rung, over and over, but it was never Jess on the line.

Now I sprinted around my room, throwing off my nightgown. I pulled on the first thing I grabbed from my closet, a faded cotton sundress. Then I ran a comb through my hair and clipped it back with two gold barrettes. Not exactly Helen of Troy, but at least I was clean. Besides, once a boy has seen you at your worst, *anything* is an improvement.

I took the stairs three at a time and swung around the oak banister and into the living room. My smile froze on my face, and my heart plummeted as I saw the boy who was talking with my mother.

"There you are." Mom smiled, looping an arm around my shoulders. "You took so long to com down that I wondered if you had heard me. Gary's been waiting for you."

Gary Quinn. I wondered if I looked as disappointed as I felt. I forced a few teeth into my smile and wiggled my fingers at the dark-haired boy sitting on the couch. "Hello, Gary. Sorry I kept you waiting. I wasn't dressed yet."

"Still lazing around in bed all morning?" Gary grinned. "Sounds like the old Chelsea we know and love. It's good to see you, Angel Face."

Angel Face . . . yucch. Suddenly the nickname that had flattered me so much before seemed terribly put-on. It was also downright embarrassing when my face was covered with mosquito bites and my mother was in the room.

"It's good to see you too," I replied, trying to instill some enthusiasm in my voice.

My mother mentioned something about checking on her Flemish tarts and tactfully disappeared. Why couldn't parents ever get it together? When you wanted them to make themselves scarce, they stuck like glue. And when you really could use a third party, they went off to fiddle with Flemish tarts.

Gary stood and walked toward me, sliding his hands into the pockets of his immaculate white pants. He looked like an ad for antiperspirant: flashing smile, sun-bronzed skin, not a hair out of place. This was the face that controlled the rhythm of half the female hearts at Skyview High. And there had been a time—one week ago, in fact—when simply looking at him had sent a little thrill through me. Before Jess.

"Were you asleep?" he asked suddenly.

"Huh? No, I wasn't asleep. Why?"

"Your face. It's all sort of . . . swollen, like you've been asleep or something."

"Mosquito bites," I explained. "I'm covered with them. It's one of the hazards of a river trip."

"Poor baby." He cupped my chin in his hand, aggravating the puffy red lumps I was trying so hard not to scratch. "You do look a little worse for the wear. I told you it was a crazy idea to go on that trip with Ranger."

My cheeks were beginning to ache from my painted-on smile. "Yes, you did."

"I'm surprised you stuck it out the whole week," Gary went on, aggravating more than just my mosquito bites. "I expected you back by Tuesday."

"In tears?" I asked lightly, pulling back from his touch. "Well, as you can see, you were wrong. I made it through the whole week without a single tear." *Forgive me, Jess.* "You know, I actually enjoyed myself. Surprised?"

"No," he drawled. "Unconvinced, but have it your way. I'll get the truth out of Ranger. So, are we still on for tonight?"

"Tonight?" I stared at him blankly.

"Yeah. I thought we'd try out the new place on Gunnison Avenue, The First Step. I hear they've got a great light show."

I had completely forgotten about our date that evening. Gary loved to dance, and ordinarily so did I. It gave me a chance to wear the silky feminine dresses I loved and to see friends I'd lost touch with during the summer. Funny how falling in love could change your outlook on things. Suddenly I realized that I would rather spend an evening with Jess tying granny knots than tripping the light fantastic with Gary Quinn.

"Gary," I said hesitantly, "would you mind if I took a rain check on tonight? I'm still pretty tired from the trip, and I'd really like an early night."

"I'll have you home by midnight," he promised. "Just like Cinderella."

Persistence. It had won him the title of Most Valuable Player on the Skyview High football team. "It's not just that," I explained. "You said yourself that my face is swollen. I'd feel like an idiot going dancing with a face full of mosquito bites."

"Not to worry." Gary pulled a pair of mirrored sunglasses from his shirt pocket and slipped them on me. "There you go. You can wear those, and no one will even know who you are. Everyone will say, "Who is that lumpy-faced girl in sunglasses dancing with that macho hunk?"

"Funny." I gave a hollow-sounding laugh and pulled off the glasses. "Really, Gary, I just don't feel up to it tonight. School starts on Monday, and I could really use the rest."

"I know school starts on Monday," Gary replied coolly. "That's why I wanted to go out with you tonight."

"I'm sorry. Maybe another time, okay?"

A muscle twitched in his cheek. "Have it your way," he said stiffly. "But I hope you don't expect me to sit home just because you want to. *I'm* not going to waste the last Saturday night before school starts."

"Why should you?" I asked. "We don't have any claims on each other, Gary."

I could tell by the expression on his handsome face that he would have been much happier if I had risen to the bait and turned green with jealousy. He muttered something about enjoying my night with Mummy and Daddy and slammed out the front door.

"Was that Gary leaving?" Mom asked, walking into the room with a plate of freshly glazed tarts. "He certainly didn't stay long. Are you two going out tonight?"

"No." I picked up one of the still-warm confections and bit into it hungrily. "We were going dancing, but I told him I was too tired. Hey, was that the phone I heard ringing a minute ago?"

"Yes. It was someone for Ranger. Why? Are you expecting a call?"

"I wish I knew." I sighed. "I wish I knew."

By the time school started on Monday, I was ready to climb the walls. It seemed that everyone in the world had either called or dropped by our house over the weekend. Neighbors, friends, even the Amway salesman. Everyone but Jess. I couldn't understand it. Even if he was still feeling under the weather, couldn't he at least have called? I didn't even have the excuse that he might have tried to reach me while I was out. I had never *gone* out. I had stayed home and waited for him to call like a lovesick schoolgirl . . . which was exactly what I was.

Sandy told me I was being impatient. "He's got to play it cool," she said. "Mark my words. He'll give it a few days, then he'll call and ask you out. Besides, haven't you heard the old expression, 'a watched pot never boils'? You sat at home and wasted your whole weekend waiting for Jess to call. If you had come with Ranger and me on Sunday like we asked you to, he would have called. That's always the way it works."

"To the boat and camper show at the Coliseum?" I shuddered, giving old locker number 28-B a kick with my foot. Immediately the door swung open. Nothing had changed since last spring. The locker I had shared with Sandy for the last three years still responded better to a kick than to a combination. "No, thank you. Even sitting home painting my toenails was more exciting than that. Now, c'mon, tell me the truth. Did you really enjoy spending the entire afternoon looking at tents and trailers?"

"Not so you'd notice it," Sandy admitted. "I really wanted to go to the pet show. My mom had two Persian cats entered, and they took first and second place. But Ranger wanted to go to the Coliseum, and I wanted to be with Ranger, so . . ." She shrugged and put her sack lunch on the top shelf of the locker.

"Boy, didn't we send the summer out with a bang?" I

closed the locker with my foot and surveyed the halls of Skyview High. The first bell had already rung, and everyone was fighting the crush to get to homeroom. "I waited for the phone to ring, and you discovered the wonderful world of recreational vehicles. I hope this doesn't get around. It could ruin our reputations."

The final bell sounded, cutting our conversation short. We ducked into the girl's rest room to check our hair and arranged to meet for lunch in the school cafeteria. I took my time climbing the two flights of stairs to English lit. As always on the first day of school, no one really expected anyone to be on time for anything. The standard excuse, "I couldn't find the room," was given at every opportunity. Wide-eyed freshmen used it out of necessity; the more intelligent (and crafty) seniors used it out of convenience. I half hoped Mr. Paulsen would ask me why I was late. I had a wonderful portrayal of a lost student lined up, complete with a quivering lower lip. But he simply rolled his eyes to the ceiling (Mr. Paulsen has been at Skyview long enough to know the ropes) and gestured toward a seat in the back of the room.

By lunchtime I felt as if I had been back at school for months. I sat in the cafeteria with my old crowd, at the same table we had been using since *we* were wide-eyed freshmen with genuine quivering lips. I listened while Kristin Shepard filled us in on her trip to Europe and commiserated with Annie Fowler over the pos-i-tive-ly boring summer she had spent at her cousin's farm in Idaho. She described her one and only attempt at milking a cow in such graphic detail that we were all in hysterics. Sandy then mentioned our river trip, and everyone's eyes swung in my direction. I felt like I had suddenly sprouted horns or something.

"What's everybody looking at me for?" I asked uncomfortably.

"We're in shock," Annie said. "Your idea of swimming is floating around on an air mattress. What on earth made you decide to go on a river trip, of all things?"

I looked around the table. My friends did indeed look as if they were in shock. It made me just the slightest bit annoyed, and I took great pleasure in describing—and exaggerating—the adventures we had had on our trip. Needless to say, my audience was spellbound. You can't imagine how wonderful it felt to impress everyone with my derring-do. I hadn't realized how boring it was being the picture of delicate femininity. I'd never put on shoulder pads and try out for the football team, but who knows? Maybe next term I would throw caution to the winds and sign up for the swim club.

Ranger caught up with us in the main hall after lunch. He had bread crumbs clinging to his pants and a wet spot on his shirt where he had spilled something. Other than that, he looked quite presentable in a white polo shirt that emphasized his broad shoulders and a pair of slim-flitting jeans. I realized with a shock that he would be almost attractive if he could learn to eat without leaving clues on his clothes.

"Have you looked outside?" he asked glumly. "I'll bet it's eighty-five degrees out there. How can they expect us to stay cooped up in a classroom on a day like this? It's inhumane."

"Cheer up." Sandy grinned and patted his arm sympathetically. "It's supposed to rain tomorrow. It'll be easier for you then."

"Why can't they hold classes out on the lawn?" he grumbled, walking down the hall between us. "At least then I could get a little fresh air. I hope Calahan realizes how lucky he is to be out of this joint. I would've given anything to have gone with them again this week."

Normally I pay very little attention to anything that my

brother says. I've learned from experience that he will either try to irritate me or bore me—or both. But at this bit of news my ears perked right up.

"Oh, did they leave on another river trip?" I asked, making an effort to sound only mildly interested.

"Yeah. This morning." He took a stick of chewing gum out of his pocket and stuffed it into his mouth.

Sandy and I exchanged a meaningful look, and I passed a silent message. I didn't want to appear too obvious. As always, Sandy understood. "Ranger, how do you know that they went on another trip?" she asked. "I thought Jess was starting college this fall."

"He ith," Ranger slurred over the wad of gum. "This is the last trip of the season. He came over last night and wanted to borrow my Springbar tent. Apparently they're taking quite a large group this time. Some sorority, I think he said."

I was so surprised that I stopped right in the middle of the hall. This was next to suicide at Skyview Hall. I nearly got trampled before Sandy pulled me back into the stream of traffic. Ranger was saying hello to a fellow football player and didn't even notice.

"Mark Howard," he said to us, as if we cared. "He's only a junior, but he's a great defensive halfback."

"What are you talking about?" I managed finally.

Ranger frowned at me. "Howard. That guy we just passed. He's a great—"

"I'm not talking about him! You said Jess came over last night."

"So what?"

What a dough head. "I was home all night," I said with exaggerated patience. "Why didn't I see him?"

"I dunno. You were in your room, I guess. It wasn't a social visit, Chelsea. The guy was just picking up the tent. He was in and out of the house in two minutes flat."

One thing at a time, I told myself calmly. This couldn't

possibly be as bad as it sounded. Last night, while I had been sitting in my room with one hand on the telephone, Jess had come over. He hadn't asked to see me or even sent a friendly hello. This morning he had left on yet another river trip. At this very moment he was a hundred miles away, tying life jackets on a bevy of beautiful sorority girls.

I was right. It wasn't as bad as it seemed. It was worse.

Ranger left us at the door of the boys' gym. Sandy and I stopped at our locker to drop off our books and walked slowly to concert choir. Neither of us spoke until we had found seats in the alto section.

I blinked away the tears in my eyes. They weren't sad tears, they were *mad* tears. What kind of games had he been playing with me, anyway? I liked him so much, and he had just been amusing himself. Obviously he had no intention of seeing me again. He had bigger fish to fry. Sorority fish.

"I'm going to look on this as a learning experience," I said through clenched teeth. "Boys are all the same. Creeps."

"Now look," Sandy said evenly, "I don't think we should jump to conclusions here."

"We aren't jumping to conclusions," I retorted. "You heard what Ranger said. Jess couldn't wait to get out of the house last night."

"He had a river trip to get ready for. Maybe he was just . . ."

"Excited?" I filled in acidly. "Considering the company he was going to have on this trip, who could blame him? Sorority girls should be a lot more fun than Boy Scouts, don't you think?"

Sandy shrugged helplessly. "I just don't get it. He seemed so sincere."

"So do rattlesnakes," I muttered.

Well, I had learned my lesson. In fact, I had learned

several lessons. It was kind of like a "good news-bad news" joke. The good news was that I had discovered an entirely new side of myself. Contrary to popular belief, I was not completely helpless. I could build a fire, pump water out of a sinking boat, and make a mean Mulligan Hash. And that was just for starters. Given enough time, who knows what I could accomplish? *Someone* should invent a truly effective mosquito repellent. The stuff I had used on the river trip had smelled like rancid tuna fish and seemed to attract the little vampires by the thousands. Maybe I could come up with something that smelled like Pavlova perfume. I could make a fortune.

And so it wasn't all bad. Okay, so I was suffering from unrequited love. Another lesson learned. Never allow your heart to rule your head. Be suspicious of anyone who calls you "princess" and wants to show you his petroglyphs. The boy you fall in love with might just run off with a group of sorority girls and break your heart.

I kept very busy during that first week of school. I signed up for two clubs, and to my friends' astonishment, I volunteered for cafeteria duty. Every day at noon I put on this little gray hair net and dished up the mystery meat of the day. My friends all thought I was doing it for a joke. Pretty soon Annie and Kristin and Sandy were standing over the steaming trays of food with me, wearing artificial flowers tucked into their hair nets and playing "name that food" with everyone who came through the line. I got into the habit of staying after school to do homework in the library, and it was usually dinnertime before I returned home. My father was thrilled that I was finally taking my schoolwork more seriously, and my mother doubled my daily dose of Flintstones vitamins so that I wouldn't get "run-down." Trying to forget Jess Calahan was very hard work.

Walking home from school on Friday, Sandy gave me something to think about besides *not* thinking about Jess.

It was a beautiful September day, and an overnight frost had left fall colors on the trees that lined Country Club Drive. I had decided to skip my after-school library session in honor of the Freshman Stomp to be held that night. It was the first social event of the school year and one of the most popular. Loudspeakers were set up in the parking lot behind the school, and the music could be heard for miles. Whether the sky was clear and filled with stars, or overcast and sprinkling snow, everyone gathered under the street-lights and danced until the midnight curfew. Unlike the more formal homecoming dance, dates were not required, and everyone came dressed in their most casual clothes. I had always figured that the sole purpose of the dance was to give everyone a chance to look everyone else over. More often than not I had come home from the Stomp in the throes of a brand-new crush, usually because some curly-haired football player had caught my eye. Considering the way Jess was sticking to my heart like a burr, I wasn't feeling too optimistic about my chances this year in the romance department. Still, anything was better than sitting home alone on a Friday night and moping.

I asked Sandy what she was going to wear, and she stared straight ahead with a grim expression. "I'm not going," she said.

I stopped dead in my tracks. A huge scarlet oak leaf floated down from the sky and rested on the pile of books I was carrying. "What do you mean, you're not going? We always go! Are you sick or something?"

"Or something," she said. "I have a date with Ranger."

She was exhibiting all the enthusiasm of a girl who had just become engaged to Jack the Ripper. I couldn't understand it. "So what's the problem?" I ran to keep up with Sandy's determined stride. "Just ask Ranger to take you to the Stomp."

"I can't," she said with a moan. "He's already bought tickets to the film."

Now I was completely baffled. "Film? What film?"

"One of those wildlife movies they show at the university. It's called *Beasts and Fowl of Botswana,* whatever that is." Sandy glanced at me meaningfully. "We have to get there early. He wants a front-row seat."

"That's not even funny," I replied, appalled at the extent of my brother's insanity. "That's disgusting. He's going to miss the best activity of the whole year to see a wildlife movie? I know he's weird, but I had no idea it had gone this far. Didn't it occur to him that you might want to go to the dance?"

"No," Sandy said simply. "He was so excited about he movie, that I don't think he even remembered about the dance. And I didn't have the heart to tell him."

"Well, someone has to tell him." I shook my head, thinking of the compromises Sandy had made over the last two weeks. "Sandy, you've done everything possible to share Ranger's interests. You went on the river trip, missed the pet show to go to that boat and camper thing at the Coliseum, and you even went to that first aid demonstration at the county library yesterday."

"It was very informative," she replied glumly. "I now know exactly what to do in case of snakebite."

"And now this! I can't believe that Ranger would be this selfish. Why, he's never even taken you on a real date!"

"That's not true," Sandy said loyally. "Last Saturday he took me out to dinner and to a movie."

"You went to McDonald's and saw *Old Yeller* at the dollar movie. That is not a date, no matter what Ranger thinks."

"He isn't trying to be selfish. I mean, he really enjoys doing all that stuff. And he thought I would enjoy it too. And I did, only . . . only I really wanted to go to the Stomp," she finished miserably.

We walked in silence until we reached Sandy's house.

All the while my little brain was clicking. Just because I was a failure with my own love life, it didn't mean that I couldn't do something to put Sandy and Captain Squirrel on the right track.

"Cheer up," I said. "Ranger is going to take you to that dance tonight or my name isn't Chelsea Hyatt. Now go make yourself gorgeous and stay close to the phone. Ranger will be calling you in about fifteen minutes."

"Chelsea, I don't want him to think—"

"He won't think anything," I said. "He never does. I'll just kind of shove him in the right direction. In fact, if it will make you feel better, I won't even let him know that I talked to you. Now go get ready and leave the rest to me."

I knew exactly where to find my predictable brother. He was in the workshop behind the garage, putting a coat of paint on an old canoe he had purchased at a swap meet. He was painting it the most horrible shade of green I had ever seen, almost the exact color of split-pea soup.

"Why did you do that?" I asked curiously.

Ranger looked up. His nose was green. "Why did I do what?"

"Paint the canoe that color. Why didn't you paint it something pretty, like blue or yellow?"

"Or pink with white polka dots?" he returned sarcastically. "I painted it green because I wanted to blend in with nature, not stick out like a sore thumb. It's called camouflage."

"It's called gross," I said sweetly. And then I put my little plan in action. "Hey, do you know what's the matter with Sandy?"

Ranger went back to his painting. "Nothing is the matter with Sandy. I saw her today at lunch and she was fine. Why?"

I shrugged. "Just wondered. When we walked home from school this afternoon, she seemed really down. Depressed. I couldn't figure it out. She's usually so excited about the Freshman Stomp. It's her favorite dance of the whole year.''

"Oh, yeah?'' Ranger frowned and put down the brush. "Did you ask her what was wrong?''

"She wouldn't talk about it. In fact, I asked her what she was going to wear tonight, and she looked like she was going to cry or something.'' I turned away and pushed the door of the shed open. "Oh, well. Maybe she just had a bad day. See you.''

"Chelsea?''

How well I knew my twin brother. I wiped the smile off my face and looked back over my shoulder. "What?''

Ranger looked very uncomfortable. And just a little bit guilty. "The Freshman Stomp . . . that's tonight?''

"Well, of course, it's tonight. Everyone knows that.''

"I didn't,'' he mumbled. "And Sandy really wanted to go, huh?''

"Like I said, it's her favorite dance of the whole year. She loves to dance.''

"Oh. I didn't know that.'' He wiped his palms on his wheat-colored cords, leaving pea-green streaks. "I never realized . . . I just figured . . . Chelsea, I'm a lousy dancer.''

I lifted my eyebrows innocently. "What's that got to do with anything?''

"Nothing.'' Ranger took a deep breath and squared his shoulders. "Look, will you clean these brushes for me? The turpentine's on the shelf in the corner. I've got a phone call to make.''

I watched Ranger jog toward the house with a satisfied smile on my face. Another career possibility. After I invented the perfect mosquito repellent, I might go into psychology. *Child* psychology.

Chapter 10

Anyone who saw me at the Freshman Stomp would have said I had a wonderful time. I arrived with Annie and Kristin in Annie's new Volkswagen Rabbit convertible. We had the top down and the radio blasting and nearly froze to death with the wind-chill factor. It did get us a lot of attention, though, which was exactly what we had in mind. I was feeling reckless and crazy, and I vowed to have a wonderful time, even if it killed me.

I had taken a lot of trouble with my appearance. I wore snug-fitting white jeans and a yellow velour top that set off my newly acquired tan. My mosquito bites were only a memory now, and my hair gleamed with the results of daily conditioning treatments. I knew exactly why it was so important for me to look my best, although I found it hard to admit. Somewhere in the back of my mind I wanted to show Jess Calahan that other boys found me attractive if he didn't. Which was insane, because Jess wouldn't even be at the Stomp, let alone care if I danced with a hundred other boys. Insanity seemed to be my password lately. My emotions kept playing games with my head, and common sense had become a thing of the past.

I danced until I got blisters on my feet, then I took off my shoes and danced some more in my stockings. I met several good-looking guys who just happened to be on the football team. I gave my phone number to a boy named John Rourke. I had noticed him in my history class because of his resemblance to Jess. He had streaky blond hair and warm brown eyes that crinkled at the corners like Jess's did when he smiled. As a matter of fact, I seemed to have Jess on the brain all night long in spite of my determined efforts to forget him. Once, when I was dancing a slow dance with Gary, I looked through the crowd and thought I saw a familiar golden-blond head. I looked again and saw redheaded Blake Dobbs dancing with a dark-haired girl I didn't know. I tried to hide the fierce stab of disappointment that shot through me. For heaven's sake, it had only taken me a week to fall in love with Jess. Why couldn't I fall out of love just as quickly?

Sandy and Ranger made their appearance a few minutes after we had arrived. Sandy was beaming and looked absolutely beautiful in a soft white sweater shot with glittering silver threads. Ranger looked uncomfortable but determined. He danced every slow dance with Sandy and glared possessively from the sidelines whenever anyone else asked her for a fast dance. Eventually jealousy triumphed over self-consciousness, and Ranger monopolized her for the rest of the evening. His style was nowhere near as polished as Sandy's, but I had to give him an *A* for effort.

As always, the last dance of the evening was slow. Gary appeared from nowhere and took me into his arms without a word, pulling me far closer than I cared to be. For one thing, he wasn't Jess. No matter how hard I pretended, no one I had met that evening measured up to Jess. And for another thing, Gary smelled like the inside of a whiskey bottle. I had no idea where he had gotten the alcohol or how much he had drunk, but his face was flushed and sweating, and his hands seemed to have a mind of their own. I practically carried him through the dance, and when it was finally over, my own face was as flushed as his. I felt like I had run a marathon. Suddenly the only thing I wanted to do was go home and cry.

"Did you bring your car?" I asked Gary tiredly.

He looked at me blankly. "Where?"

This was worse than I had thought. Not only was he drunk, but his face had taken on the color of Ranger's canoe. "To the dance," I said patiently, enunciating each word, as if I were teaching the alphabet to a child. "Did you bring your car or did someone drive you here?"

"Brought my car," he said thickly. He ran a hand through his dark hair and looked up and down the street. "It's here somewhere. Want a ride home, Angel Face?"

I scanned the rapidly thinning crowd for Sandy and Ranger, but they were nowhere in sight. It seemed that I was on my own. I sighed and put an arm around Gary's waist to support him. "Sure," I said. "On one condition. I get to drive."

Sober, Gary Quinn never would have considered letting a mere female drive his beloved car. Tonight he just shrugged and said, "Why not? You know how to drive a stick shift?"

"Of course I do." I crossed my fingers behind my back. "Everyone knows how to drive standard. Wait here while I find Annie and tell her I'm going with you."

It was nearly one o'clock in the morning by the time we found his car. He had parked it in an alley almost two blocks down the street. Gary apologized for forgetting where he had parked, then slumped down in the seat and appeared to fall fast asleep. I buckled him in like a baby, then took a deep breath and slid into the driver's seat.

It was stop-and-go for a while. Literally. Every time I shifted gears, the car made a terrible grinding noise and the engine died. Finally I solved the problem by leaving the car in first gear and driving along at a steady nine miles an hour. Gary lived less than a mile from my house. I figured I would drive him home, then walk the rest of the way to my house. I wasn't exactly crazy about walking home alone in the dark, but I didn't see what choice I had. If I called my father for a ride, he'd be bound to get the whole story out of me. I had never seen Gary drink before, and I hated to be the one to blow the whistle on him now. It was going to be hard enough explaining to my parents why I was getting home an hour later than my usual Friday-night curfew.

I took the long way home, taking the winding residential streets to avoid clogging traffic on the main roads. When the car suddenly began lurching up and down, I was baffled. It felt like I was driving over an obstacle course of bowling balls. I had trouble steering, and it took all my strength to pull over to the side of the road.

Gary opened his eyes when I cut the engine. "Whasamatter? We home already?"

"No, we're not home. There's something the matter with your stupid car!"

Instantly he was wide-awake and, apparently, cold sober. "My car? What did you do to it? Did you run into something?"

I felt like screaming. What had I done to deserve this? Now it would be even later when I got home. My parents were probably pacing the living room this very minute, thinking up cruel and unusual punishments for me. "Gary, I don't know what's wrong. I didn't hit anything, and I was driving very carefully." How reckless could you be when you were stuck in first gear? "It just started . . . limping all of a sudden. And it pulled to the left when I tried to steer it."

"Limping," Gary repeated sarcastically. "Oh, that helps a lot."

He grabbed a flashlight from the glove compartment. I got out of the driver's side and slammed the car door. He slammed the door on the passenger side and walked slowly around the car.

"There it is." He directed the weak yellow beam at the left rear tire. "Flat as a pancake. You must have run over a nail or something."

"Oh, forgive me," I replied scathingly. "How could I have been so careless?"

Gary clamped down his teeth on whatever reply he had been about to make. He walked to the trunk of the car—he was still rather unsteady on his feet—and pulled out a tire jack and a crowbar. He tossed me the flashlight, and I had to jump sideways to catch it.

"Hold it," he said curtly, "so I can see what I'm doing."

After ten minutes he still hadn't managed to pry the hubcap off. His fingers were stiff and clumsy, and he seemed to be moving in slow motion. It was obvious that he was still more than half drunk. It was also clear that we would never get home unless I either changed the tire myself or started walking. Since I had never changed a tire in my life, I decided on the latter.

"I'm going to walk home," I announced. I clicked off the flashlight and dropped it through the car window. "You can stay here and swear at the hubcap, or you can come with me. I don't really care."

"We can't just leave my car here all night!"

"I can," I said shortly. "It's not my car."

"And what do I tell my dad when he wants to know where my car is?"

"Tell him the truth!" I was practically yelling now. "Tell him you had a flat tire and were too drunk to get the stupid hubcap off!"

We were glaring at each other when suddenly a car came around the bend, its headlights blinding us. I heard the tires spitting gravel as the car pulled sharply to the right, coming to a halt directly behind Gary's Trans-Am. The driver turned off the motor but left the headlights on. The car door slammed violently, and I held my breath.

I had expected a policeman or perhaps my father. That would have been bad enough. When Jess Calahan walked into the light, I was stunned.

He was angry. I had never seen Jess this angry before. His golden eyes glittered like ice, and his jaw was set in stone. There was still a faint shadow under his left eye, I noticed dumbly. Apparently his shiner had taken a long time to heal. From the way Jess was looking at Gary, I thought he might be considering passing the black eye on to him. Then he turned the same gaze on me and I gulped.

"I thought it was you," he said. In his voice I could hear the restrained violence of a tightly checked temper. "Isn't it past your bedtime, princess?"

"Who the heck are you?" Gary demanded. "Chelsea, you know this guy?"

I prayed that the ground would open up and swallow me. Gary's slurred speech made his condition painfully cleare. This ddid not look good for me. "I know him," I managed huskily. "He is a . . . friend of mine."

"Oh." Gary seemed to take this at face value. "Hey, you wanna help us out of here? We've got a flat tire, and Chelsea's having fits about getting home."

Jess looked at me for a long moment. I could see a muscle working in his cheek. Then he brushed past me and took the crowbar out of Gary's hand. While he changed the tire Gary shuffled around on the gravel, offering advice and in general being completely useless. Within ten minutes Jess had the spare tire on. He threw the tire jack, crowbar, and punctured tire into the trunk of the car and turned to Gary. "Where are your keys?"

"In the car," Gary said. "Hey, look, everything's cool. I had a few too many, but I'm fine now."

Jess smiled—sort of. "You think so?"

"Yeah, I think so!" Gary's jaw thrust out belligerently.

"I appreciate your help, but I can handle things now. C'mon, Chelsea. Get in the car and I'll drive you home."

"No, you won't," Jess said coldly. "Man, you couldn't even change a tire, let alone drive a car. I'll drive you. Chelsea can follow us to your house in my car."

"Now look," Gary began, but he was cut short when Jess caught his shirtfront in a crushing grip.

"You look, buddy. No way is this girl getting in a car with you. I'm not in a very good mood right now, so just shut up and *get in the car.*"

Apparently something in Jess's face convinced Gary that he would be better off doing as he was told. Keeping his face averted, he walked around the car and got in the passenger side. Jess looked at me as if he expected an argument. I held his eyes for a moment, then shrugged and walked over to his car. It was an old white Ford equipped with—thank heaven—an automatic transmission. I drove carefully, trailing the gleaming black Trans-Am the few miles to Gary's house. I pulled over to the curb and waited with the engine idling while Jess parked Gary's car in the driveway. Seconds later Jess pulled open the door on the driver's side and motioned for me to slide over.

"Where's Gary?" I asked. "Is he okay?"

"No. Right now he's doubled over behind the evergreens, regretting every drop he drank."

"I can't leave him like that!" I moved to open the car door. Jess swore softly and reached in front of me, slamming the lock down on the door.

"Just leave him alone," he ordered grimly. "The last thing he needs is an audience while he's sick. He's going to be humiliated enough in the morning. Do up your seat belt."

"I don't need a seat belt. It's all of one mile to my house from here." Even to my ears I sounded like a tired, irritable child.

A loaded silence followed. When Jess finally spoke, his

voice was deceptively mild. "Your parents never spanked
you when you were little, did they? I didn't think so. Do up
your seat belt, princess. *Now.*"

I buckled my seat belt and subsided into a brooding
silence. Not a word was spoken until Jess pulled into our
driveway. I had heard of companionable silences, and this
definitely was not one of them. The tension in the car
could be cut with a knife.

I was relieved to see only the porch light burning. Maybe
I had lucked out after all. Mom and Dad might have gone
to sleep instead of waiting up for me. I was certainly due
for a break.

"Thank you," I said stiffly, avoiding Jess's eyes. "I
appreciate your help with the tire. We're lucky you happened to come along."

"Really?" he drawled. "I thought maybe I was . . .
interrupting."

"It's not what you think," I whispered over the con-
striction in my throat.

"And how do you know what I'm thinking?" he
responded coolly. "Are you reading minds now,
princess?"

I wouldn't cry. I *wouldn't*. If he wanted to think the
worst, then let him. Why should I try to explain? I fumbled
with the door handle, feeling the heat build in my cheeks.
How could I make a dignified exit when I couldn't even get
out of the stupid car?

"The lock," Jess said.

I unlocked the door, unbuckled my seat belt, and
climbed out of the car. Tears burned my eyes, and I
slashed at them with one of my fists. It was a pity that I
hadn't developed the ability to *stop* crying at will. It would
have been very useful about now.

Jess said something that sounded like "Take care." I
ran into the house without another word, partly because I

didn't want him to see me cry, and partly because I didn't know what else to do.

My parents weren't waiting up for me. My brother was. He sat on the couch in the living room with a bag of Fig Newtons for company. The only light in the room came from the flickering television set in the corner. Bella Lugosi smiled at me with gleaming vampire fangs. *I want to suck your blood. . . .*

"The Curse of Count Dracula," Ranger informed me, holding out the Fig Newtons. "Have a cookie."

"No, thanks." I had to clear my throat twice before the words came out. "Mom and Dad asleep?"

"Yeah. I told them I would wait up for you. Watch this. That priest is going to get pushed off the roof."

Just what I needed. "I'm tired. I'm going up to bed."

"You want to talk about it?" he asked quietly.

I stared at him. "Talk about what?"

"Why you've been crying." Another Fig Newton disappeared in one gulp. "Why you're coming in at two in the morning. Why you look like you've been dragged through a rabbit hole backward."

I looked down at my clothes. They were wrinkled and streaked with grease. My white pants would never be the same. "Mom's going to have a fit," I mumbled.

"I get the feeling I should be out punching someone in the nose for you," Ranger said mildly. "I didn't recognize the car in the driveway just now. Who brought you home?"

"Jess." I barely whispered the word.

Ranger looked pained. "I was afraid you'd say that. He's bigger than I am."

"Oh, shut up." I sank down beside him on the couch. "You know Jess better than that."

"Yeah, I do. So why don't you tell me what's going on?"

In between cookies I explained everything that had happened. Ranger listened quietly, choking a little bit when I described the difficulties I had had driving Gary's car. I managed to keep the tears at bay until I repeated the comment Jess had made about "interrupting" Gary and me. What else could he think, after all? There we were at two o'clock in the morning, parked on a quiet side street with Gary reeking of alcohol. Even the flat tire hadn't convinced Jess that nothing was going on.

But why should I care what Jess thought? I asked myself angrily. It wasn't as if we were going together. We had never even been out on a date. He had made absolutely no effort to see me since the river trip. There was no reason in the world why his opinion of me should matter one way or the other.

But it did.

Ranger stuffed a wad of tissues in my hands. "You and Old Faithful," he said dryly. "Well, I guess I won't go punch Gary in the nose. It sounds like you ruined the transmission on his car. That's punishment enough."

"He was sick too."

"That'll teach him. It only takes once. I'll never forget the hangover I had when—" He broke off, coloring under his tan. "Never mind," he said hastily. "You never did tell me what Jess was doing around here so late at night."

"He didn't tell me," I sniffed, "and I didn't ask. He was probably on his way home from a big date."

"He just got back from the river trip this afternoon. I don't think he'd have a 'big date' the same night."

I blew my nose. "I guess it would depend"—hiccup—"on who he met during the river trip, wouldn't it?"

Ranger blinked at me. "*Now* what are you talking about?"

"Sorority girls," I said darkly. "You told me yourself

he was taking a group of sorority girls on the river trip."

"So I did." He sighed and scratched his head. "Look, sis, I don't think you need to worry—"

"Worry? I'm not worried." I busied myself gathering up the shredded tissues. "What Jess does or doesn't do is no concern of mine. I'm just sorry things turned out the way they did tonight. It was a little embarrassing, that's all. And tiring. I'm going to bed."

"You'll miss the rest of the movie," Ranger warned me. "That guy with the wooden stake is about to put an end to Dracula."

"Sounds original." Suddenly I realized how very tired I was. My eyes felt like they were filled with sand, and my arms and legs seemed weighted with lead. It was an effort just to walk over to the stairs. "You can tell me all about it in the morning. Hey, Ranger?"

"Yeah?"

"How did it go with you and Sandy tonight?"

He grinned and flopped lengthwise onto the couch. "The girl," he said simply, "is smitten."

I barely managed to change into my nightgown before I dropped into bed. When I woke up the next morning, I discovered that I was still wearing the dirty socks I had danced in the night before. I could hear the lawn mower roaring in the backyard and a neighbor's dog barking. I blinked at the clock on my nightstand until it came into focus. I had exactly eighteen minutes to make it to the Burger Barn before my twelve-o'clock shift.

I do not work at the Burger Barn for the money. No one works at the Burger Barn for the money. They only pay minimum wage, and if the teenage customers leave any tip, it's always something cute like a dime dropped in a half-empty glass of Coke. I only work on Saturdays from noon to four, which happens to be the busiest time of the whole week. Everyone from school seems to drop by the Burger

Barn on Saturday afternoons. It's a great place to see people, and working there offers a funny kind of prestige.

I arrived fifteen minutes late. The rush had already begun, and for three hours I took orders and counted change and carried little plastic trays back and forth to the crowded tables. Normally I enjoyed the fast pace and the banter tossed back and forth, but normally I didn't have blisters all over my feet. Toward the end of my shift I was limping, first on one foot, then on the other. Every step was agony, and I wondered if the Board of Health would condemn the Burger Barn if I took off my shoes.

It was nearly four o'clock when I noticed Gary Quinn walk in and sit down at one of the booths. He had huge, dark circles under his eyes and a strange yellow tinge to his skin. He caught my eye and tried out an uncertain smile. Silently he mouthed the words, *I need to talk to you.*

It would have taken a heart of stone to resist his appeal. Poor Gary looked absolutely terrible. I could practically hear the hammers pounding in his head.

Fortunately the girl who was supposed to take over for me arrived early. I don't think my feet would have survived another ten minutes. I punched out my time card and shuffled over to Gary's booth, sliding onto the vinyl bench across from him. Immediately I slipped my feet out of my shoes.

"Are you okay?" Gary asked, frowning. "You're walking kind of funny."

"I learned a lesson last night," I said. "People with tender feet should never spend an entire night dancing. I guess I'm not cut out for life in the fast lane."

Gary looked down at his hands clasped on the table. "I learned something too. People with tender heads should stay away from alcohol. Chelsea, I'm really sorry about last night. Some guy had a keg behind the bleachers, and I guess I got in line once too often. The next thing I knew, I was facedown in the fitzers."

"Are you all right now?" I asked hesitantly. "You don't look so good."

He grimaced. "I don't feel so good. Believe me, it's the last time I'll try a stunt like that. Chelsea . . . what happened when you got home last night? Were your parents angry?"

I knew Gary well enough to realize that his concern was probably more for his own hide than mine. Mr. Quinn and Dad played golf together every week. If I had spilled the beans last night, Gary's parents would have been sure to find out.

"Don't worry," I said dryly. "You're in the clear. Mom and Dad were both asleep when I got home. Ranger was waiting up for me, but he isn't going to say anything."

Gary heaved a sigh of relief. "Wow. You don't know how glad I am to hear that. Are we friends again, Angel Face?"

Trying to dislike Gary was like trying to dislike a dim-witted puppy dog. It was impossible. I nodded my head and smiled. "Friends."

Out of the corner of my eye I saw Ranger coming through the door. I waved at him, then my hand froze. Likewise my breathing and my heart. Jess stood behind Ranger, looking straight at me without a flicker of emotion. I might have been a chair or a table or a painted menu on the wall. He tapped Ranger on the shoulder and pointed to a booth that had just been vacated.

"You need a ride home?" Gary asked.

"No, thanks." My voice was lifeless. "I have my mom's car."

"So do I." He grinned. "Mine's in the shop having the transmission repaired."

Chapter 11

On Monday I woke up with a sore throat. I took three vitamin C pills with breakfast and went to school, anyway. By Wednesday morning I was really sick: hot one minute, cold the next, with every bone in my body aching and my nose running like a stream. Before she left for work, Mom tucked me into bed like a sick toddler and brought the vaporizer into my room. By the time she got home, the whole house smelled like a eucalyptus tree and I had used up an entire box of tissues.

The doctor said that I had a simple cold and that I should drink plenty of fluids, etcetera, etcetera. I preferred to think that I had a terrible disease and was clinging to life only by sheer determination. I always got dramatic when I didn't feel well.

I drank chicken broth until the very smell of it turned me green. Dad moved the television set into my room, and I watched soap operas eight hours a day. I became an addict. The hazards of a river trip were nothing compared to life in a soap opera.

By Saturday, I was up and wandering around the house in my bunny slippers. I didn't feel well enough to go out, and I felt too good to lay around in bed. Mom and Dad, reassured by the doctor that I was well on the road to recovery, had gone to spend the weekend in Aspen with friends. Ranger had left before dawn to go fishing. I called Sandy, but her mother was afraid she would catch my cold if she came over. There were no soap operas aired on Saturday, so I spent the entire afternoon watching Celebrity Bowling and eating butter-brickle ice cream.

I was back in my room playing Solitaire when I heard Ranger slam the front door. Several more slamming doors followed, along with various thuds and crashes that I couldn't identify. The message was very clear, though— *no fish.*

Ranger stomped up the stairs and stood in the doorway, chewing on a cold chicken leg. He smelled like a fish, but I had learned long ago that this had no bearing on whether he had actually caught any fish.

"Have a nice day?" I asked sweetly.

"No. It was freezing, the fish have all gone into hibernation, and I got a hook caught in the seat of my pants. It was not a nice day."

I put a red six on a red seven. It was cheating, but I was bored and wanted to end the game. "Serves you right. You shouldn't have left your poor sick sister home alone all day. I could have died, and no one even would have known."

"Only if you sneezed yourself to death." He sat on the edge of the bed, and all the cards tumbled out of their piles. "But I'll tell you, if I had know what kind of a mood Jess was going to be in, I would have stayed home. Even listening to you whine and sniff would have been better than spending the day with him."

"Oh, yeah?" I did my best to appear nonchalant. "I didn't know you went with Jess. What was the matter with him?"

"He was like a bear with a sore foot. He never smiled,

never talked . . . he wouldn't even fish. All he did was skip stones across the river all day. What's that smell in here?"

"It's you."

"No, the medicine smell."

"Oh. It's probably the Vicks. Keeps my nose clear."

Ranger chewed noisily on the chicken. He seemed preoccupied with his thoughts. I brushed all the cards off my bed with a sweep of my hand. Solitaire was boring. It would have been fun to play Fish or Concentration but only with the right partner. . . .

"I need your advice," Ranger said suddenly.

"I've been watching *General Hospital*," I said cheerfully, thinking that he and Sandy might have had a fight. "I can advise you on anything."

"I'm not the one with the problem," he explained. "It's my friend."

"Ahhh . . . your friend."

"Yeah. See, he told me he really likes this girl. The problem is, he thinks she is too good for him. She comes from a pretty wealthy family, lives in a nice house . . . did I mention that he met her on a river trip?"

I had suddenly lost my voice. I shook my head dumbly.

"Well, he did. Anyway, this friend is feeling pretty bad about the whole thing. Besides, he thinks she likes someone else, someone more in her league. So he's decided that the best thing he can do for this girl is stay out of her life. Did I mention that she was homecoming princess last year?"

"No . . ."

"Well, she was. And like I said, this friend is feeling pretty cut up about her. In fact, he's miserable. I kept thinking that they would work things out by themselves, but now I'm not so sure. I don't know what to do about it."

"Maybe you ought to tell the girl about all this," I

whispered. "If she likes him as much as he likes her, she would probably want to know."

"Can't do that." Ranger shook his head and chucked the naked chicken bone into the garbage can. "I promised my friend that I would never say anything about this to her. He's pretty sensitive about the fact that he hasn't got much money. He's working two part-time jobs just to put himself through school. And you know me, sis. I always keep my promises." He stood up and stretched. "Oh, well. Just talking about things like this helps. It kind of sets your thinking straight, you know what I mean? 'Night, Chelsea."

Long after he had left, I sat frozen on my bed. I replayed in my mind every word Ranger had uttered, just to be sure. It never occurred to me that he wasn't telling the truth. Ranger didn't have the imagination to make up a story like that. No, everything fit. The whole complete muddled mess suddenly made sense.

I realized that my mouth was hanging open. I closed it. I was dizzy with surprise, elated with the most wonderful heart-in-the-throat feeling. He cared. That stubborn, proud, hardheaded idiot cared as much about me as I did about him.

Now what was I going to do?

It took me three days to completely recover from my cold. It took me another two days after that to get up my courage. Immediately after school on Friday I caught the bus that went to the university. Courtesy of another round-about talk with Ranger, I had discovered that Jess worked in the college bookstore every Monday and Friday until five o'clock. When I got off the bus at the south end of the campus, it was four-thirty.

I inquired at the administration building, and they told me that the bookstore was at the north end of the campus.

I half ran and half walked and prayed that the directions I had been given were accurate. I wasn't at all familiar with the university, and it seemed like a bewildering maze of buildings and walkways.

It was two minutes before five when I finally walked into the bookstore. It was far bigger than I had imagined, with an open stairwell that ran from the ground floor to the second and third levels. I spotted Jess immediately. He was standing behind the cash register, blessing two lucky co-eds with *that smile.* I would have turned and fled then and there if he hadn't looked up at that very moment. He spotted me, and his eyes pinned me against the wall.

For the barest second his guard slipped. It was all there in his golden eyes, the wanting and needing that I knew was reflected in my own. His smile wobbled on his face, and one of the co-eds had to shake his arm to get his attention.

It was all that I needed. I picked a book at random from the shelves—it turned out to be *Partridge's Dictionary of Abbreviations*—and stood in line behind the cash register. The girl in front of me tried to strike up a conversation with Jess. She was tall, blond, and giggly, and looked curvy even from the back. Jess seemed to look right through her, which I thought was probably a good sign.

I put my book on the counter and pulled my wallet out of my purse.

"You're kidding," Jess said. "You don't really want this . . . do you?"

"Of course I do. Why else would I come in here?"

He looked completely baffled but began punching numbers in on the cash register.

"You don't think I'd come here just to see you, do you?" I went on innocently. "Don't worry, you've made it perfectly clear how you feel about me. I wouldn't embarrass you by *chasing* you anything."

"I wouldn't be embarrassed," said the boy behind me cheerfully. "You can chase me anytime."

"Four fifty-six," Jess said blankly.

I pulled a five-dollar bill out of my wallet. Thank goodness I had some money. I hadn't even thought to check. "I guess I made it pretty obvious how I felt about you, but I'll get over it. I'm mature enough to understand that just because you like a person doesn't necessarily mean they're going to return those feelings."

"I'll help you get over it," the boy behind me offered. "The best thing is to keep busy. What are you doing tonight?"

"After all"—I smiled at Jess—"you either like someone or you don't, right? It doesn't matter what kind of clothes they wear or what kind of house they live in. It's what's inside that counts."

"I couldn't agree with you more," said the voice over my shoulder. "My name's Fred, by the way."

Jess slammed the cash register shut. "Back off, Fred. You're irritating me."

"That's one of the things I admire about you," I told Jess. "You're so *honest*. You would never look down on a person because they might be poor, any more than you would avoid someone because they might be wealthy. One thing is as bad as the other, don't you think? Either way you're a snob."

"Chelsea . . . I never—"

"I'm holding up the line," I said quickly. "I'd better go. It's been nice seeing you again, Jess. Tell Mike hello."

I grabbed my book and my purse and walked quickly out of the store. I followed the shaded cobblestone pathway that wound through the campus, walked beneath the arches of the student union building, and entered a sunlit courtyard where a huge fountain threw water some thirty feet in the air. I had no idea where the bus might be. I was hopelessly lost.

I turned to the person closest to me to ask for directions. "Excuse me. Could you please—"

"Could I please what?" Jess asked politely. His hair was tangled over his forehead as if he had been running, but he didn't seem to be breathing hard. And I didn't seem to be breathing at all. My confidence had deserted me, along with my power of speech.

"You," I managed finally.

"Fred wanted to come," Jess explained, "but I told him you were taken. Permanently."

I tried to swallow but couldn't. "And when did that happen?"

Jess's head tilted slightly as he studied me, a slow smile creasing his cheeks. "I'm not sure," he said thoughtfully. "Probably the first time I fished you out of the Colorado. Or it might have been when I watched you build your first fire or when you got all tangled up in the twine trying to tie a barrel knot. You're a very hard girl not to love."

"Love?" I repeated shakily.

"Love." He nodded, running a hand over my hair. "Don't you know how much I care about you, princess?"

"You didn't act like it. You never came by, never called—"

"I was being noble." He grinned. "Noble and stupid. I guess I needed a few days to sort things out in my mind."

"And did you?"

"That depends." Jess took my hand and led me over to the fountain. We sat down on the wide stone ledge next to a bearded hippie-type who was playing a flute. He wore a red bandana on his head, had a butterfly tattoo on his arm, and seemed oblivious to the world around him. He also played the most beautiful music I had ever heard.

"Depends on what?" I asked softly.

For the first time Jess looked away, squinting into the sunlight. "On you. And Gary."

"Gary?" I frowned. "What about Gary?"

"That's what I'd like to know. I went to the Stomp Friday night, and the first thing I saw was you dancing with him."

"Then it was you I saw," I said slowly. "I thought my mind was playing tricks on me."

"Oh, I was there, all right. I watched Gary ducking behind the bleachers every fifteen minutes for refreshments. I knew he was drunk, so I decided I'd better follow you home. It wasn't by chance that I stopped to help you."

"But you seemed so angry," I ventured cautiously.

"I was. I was so jealous, I wanted to slug somebody." His smile widened. "I showed terrific self-control, don't you think?"

"Terrific," I said dryly. "Especially when you took me home."

"I didn't know how you felt about me," Jess said quietly. "I thought you liked Gary. What else could I do?"

Very carefully I put my purse and book on the ledge. Then I put my arms around his neck and pulled his face close to mine. "Ask me," I whispered. "Ask me how I feel about you."

Jess took a deep breath and rested his forehead against mine. "Chelsea Hyatt . . . how do you feel about me?"

"I love you," I said, gazing into the sun-filled eyes that had grown intensely solemn. "You're stubborn and opinionated and too proud for your own good, but I love you, anyway."

It would have been a storybook ending. A romantic kiss in front of a sparkling fountain, complete with flute music in the background. It *would* have been, if we hadn't overbalanced and tumbled backward into the water. We sruggled to our feet, dripping and clutching each other and listening to the applause of the students who had gathered for the show.

"Nothing," Jess said, groaning, "*nothing* works out the way I planned with you."

"I know." I staggered to keep my balance. "It's a good sign, don't you think? You'll never be bored with me."

He began to laugh. Then he kissed me, right in front of the goldfish and everybody. Our audience clapped and whistled, and when that long, wonderful kiss was over, Jess and I held tightly to each other's hand and took a bow.

About the Author

Tonya Wood is a native of Salt Lake City, Utah. She is married and has five young children who provide her with a constant form of aerobic exercise. She describes herself as an "incurable romantic" and loves camping with her family in the beautiful Rocky Mountains. This is her first novel.

Super Tales for Teens from Vista

(0451)

☐ **SAILBOAT SUMMER by Anne Reynolds.** Mackenzie thought she was in for a boring, boyless summer, until school basketball star Craig Lawson, and her best friend's cute cousin Kurt both invite her to go sailing. But dating two good-looking guys at once turned out to be real trouble, especially when she had to choose between them ... (123492—$1.95)

☐ **MEET SUPER DUPER RICK MARTIN by Judith Enderle.** Rick's new at Lawrence High and to Annie he's G-O-R-G-E-O-U-S! Only Linda has eyes for him too, and unlike Annie *she* knows how to bat them, *she* knows how to flirt. But Annie's best friend has a plan to get them together that seems foolproof, but is it? (138686—$2.50)

☐ **JULIE'S MAGIC MOMENT by Barbara Bartholomew.** Julie had never been popular before, but now that she has the lead in the fall play at her new school, everybody wants to know her. As long as she played the roles these new friends expected, Julie would be popular— but what if she stopped pretending? (126289—$2.25)

☐ **SMART GIRL by Sandy Miller.** Now that she was a senior in high school, Elizabeth Ellen, "E.E." to her friends, was getting tired of being seen only as the class brain. Then she met handsome Bruce Johnson, and when he asked her out, she realized that though she was bright in school she had a lot to learn about people. (118871—$2.25)

Prices slightly higher in Canada

Buy them at your local bookstore or use this convenient coupon for ordering.

NEW AMERICAN LIBRARY,
P.O. Box 999, Bergenfield, New Jersey 07621

Please send me the books I have checked above. I am enclosing $_____
(please add $1.00 to this order to cover postage and handling). Send check or money order—no cash or C.O.D.'s. Prices and numbers are subject to change without notice.

Name _____

Address_____

City_____State_____Zip Code_____
Allow 4-6 weeks for delivery.
This offer is subject to withdrawal without notice.